Deep-Sea Treasury

SHARK SCHOOL

Deep-Sea Treasury

Books #1-4

DEEP-SEA DISASTER · LIGHTS! CAMERA! HAMMERHEAD! ·
SQUID-NAPPED! · THE BOY WHO CRIED SHARK

BY DAVY OCEAN
ILLUSTRATED BY AARON BLECHA

ALADDIN   New York   London   Toronto   Sydney   New Delhi

WITH THANKS TO PAUL EBBS

ALADDIN
An imprint of Simon & Schuster Children's Publishing Division
1230 Avenue of the Americas, New York, New York 10020
This Aladdin hardcover edition March 2015
Text copyright © 2013 by Hothouse Fiction
Deep-Sea Disaster text copyright © 2013 by Hothouse Fiction
Deep-Sea Disaster illustrations copyright © 2013 by Aaron Blecha
Originally published in Great Britain by Templar Publishing.
Lights! Camera! Hammerhead! text copyright © 2013 by Hothouse Fiction
Lights! Camera! Hammerhead! illustrations copyright © 2013 by Aaron Blecha
Originally published in Great Britain by Templar Publishing.
Squid-napped! text copyright © 2013 by Hothouse Fiction
Squid-napped! illustrations copyright © 2013 by Aaron Blecha
Originally published as *Lone Shark* in Great Britain by Templar Publishing.
The Boy Who Cried Shark text copyright © 2013 by Hothouse Fiction
The Boy Who Cried Shark illustrations copyright © 2013 by Aaron Blecha
Originally published as *Harry Hammer: Shark Alert* in Great Britain by Templar Publishing.
All rights reserved, including the right of reproduction in whole or in part in any form.
ALADDIN is a trademark of Simon & Schuster, Inc., and related logo
is a registered trademark of Simon & Schuster, Inc.
For information about special discounts for bulk purchases, please contact
Simon & Schuster Special Sales at 1-866-506-1949 or business@simonandschuster.com.
The Simon & Schuster Speakers Bureau can bring authors to your live event.
For more information or to book an event contact the Simon & Schuster Speakers Bureau
at 1-866-248-3049 or visit our website at www.simonspeakers.com.
Cover designed by Karin Paprocki
Interior designed by Mike Rosamilia
The text of this book was set in Write Demibd
Manufactured in the United States of America 0217 FFG
4 6 8 10 9 7 5 3
ISBN 978-1-4814-5115-4
ISBN 978-1-4814-0680-2 (*Deep-Sea Disaster* eBook)
ISBN 978-1-4814-0683-3 (*Lights! Camera! Hammerhead!* eBook)
ISBN 978-1-4814-0686-4 (*Squid-napped!* eBook)
ISBN 978-1-4814-0690-1 (*The Boy Who Cried Shark* eBook)
This title has been cataloged with the Library of Congress.
These titles were previously published individually by Aladdin.

Contents

Deep-Sea Disaster

CHAPTER 1

I'm having my favorite dream again—
the one where I'm about to be crowned
Greatest Underwater Wrestling Champion of the World, Ever. I swim up to
the top rope of the ring and prepare to
launch.

"I think he's going for a dropflick!"

a jellyfish commentator shouts into his microphone.

"There's no stopping this hammer-head shark tonight," adds his partner, a bright orange clown fish.

"Har-ry! Har-ry!" the crowd begins to chant.

One diving dropflick and the blue shark I'm fighting will be fish food and the underwater wrestling belt will be mine. I dive down from the rope and pin my opponent to the canvas.

"Har-ry! Har-ry!" The crowd's voices get louder and louder. And louder. And then too loud. Like they are shouting right in my ear.

Underwater Wrestling Champion of the World to having to get ready for school, in less than ten seconds.

"So, are you awake, then?"

"Yes!"

"Cool. See you tomorrow."

"Can't wait."

Humphrey swims off out the window to go and get his breakfast.

I swivel my right eye around until I can see the huge poster of Gregor the Gnasher hanging on the rocky wall at the end of my bed. Gregor the Gnasher is the *actual* Underwater Wrestling Champion of the World. In

the poster, he's holding his winner's belt high above his head and smiling so widely you can see all of his 3,017 teeth.

Gregor is a great white shark and as well as his rows and rows of razor-sharp teeth, he has a long pointed snout and a humongous body. He's exactly what a shark *should* look like. And he's scary. Super scary. Even my poster of him makes my pet catfish poop itself.

If they made a poster of me, my catfish would probably just laugh. You see, I'm a hammerhead shark, which, for those of you who haven't already figured it out,

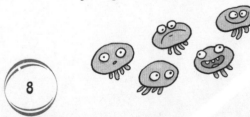

means I have a head that's the shape of a hammer. With goggly eyes so far apart they look like they don't even talk to each other. It's not a great look. Espe-

cially if you want to be taken seriously in the shark world.

I once made a list of the five coolest sharks in existence. It went like this:

1. The great white–obviously.

2. The blue shark–
the fastest fish in
the sea.

3. The tiger shark–
scary and stripy.

4. The whale shark–
its mouth is so huge
it can swallow a
dolphin in one gulp!

5. The bull shark–
it can swim in
rivers as well as
the sea, which is
very handy if you're
going on vacation and stuff.

You may have noticed that the hammerhead shark isn't on the list. That's because the hammerhead shark is seriously uncool. In fact, the only shark less cool than a hammerhead is the nurse shark. Nurse sharks are the girliest sharks in the ocean—which is fine if you're a girl and everything, but I'm not.

Gregor doesn't just look cool, he can do lots of cool stuff too. Then I have an idea. I might not look like Gregor, but that doesn't mean I can't *be* like him. I swim out of bed and over to the old treasure chest where I keep my collection of shells shaped like famous sports

stars and all my lists. I once made a list of all the cool stuff Gregor can do. I take it out and study it.

Number one is out, obviously.

1. Wrestling—he's the Underwater Champion ten years running.

2. Eating boats—which scares the life out of the leggy air-breathers.

3. Looking really mean—without even trying.

4. Swimming fast—as fast as any speedboat.

5. Ambushing prey—they never see him coming.

You can't just be Underwater Wrestling Champion of the World in, like, two weeks or something. It takes years of deep-sea training: weight-lifting anchors, eating high-energy seaweed bars, and swimming laps around ocean liners.

Number two is a no-no as well. First of all, my mouth is way too small. Sometimes I find it hard swallowing a crab. Also, I'm not allowed up to the surface without one of my parents being with me. I know that sounds really lame—I mean, I'm ten years old. What do they think I'm going to do? Go sunbathing on the beach?

And I'm not going to eat any strange food dangling from fishing lines either. Everyone knows what fishermen do to sharks when they catch them. They make their fins into soup, that's what. And there's no way I'd risk losing my fins. Imagine what a laughingstock I'd be then, with a head like a hammer and a body like an eel!

I put on my school tie and blazer and then read number three on my list: *Looking really mean*. Hmm, now that sounds a bit easier. And if I looked really mean, certain sharks might not make fun of me anymore. I swim over to my mirror and scrunch my eyes shut. Then I make my

meanest face. I imagine I'm giving the sort of scary scowl that Gregor makes when he's entering the wrestling ring. It feels pretty good. I can already imagine Rick Reef and his goofy sidekick, Donny Dogfish, taking one look at the new me and speeding off to hide behind the school cafeteria.

But when I open my eyes and look in the mirror, I don't see the mean monster of my dreams—and Rick Reef's nightmares—I see a schoolkid who looks like he's having trouble making a poop!

I swim back to the list, feeling a bit worried. I'm starting to run out of options. Okay, number four: *Swimming fast.* I'm not bad at this, actually, but I'm not clueless—I'm never going to be as fast as Gregor. I look at number five: *Ambushing prey.* Aha—now, surely I can do that. I mean, how hard can it be? I scan my bedroom, looking for a victim. My eyes come to rest upon Lenny, my lantern fish, snoozing away above my desk, his antennae glowing softly in the dark. Being careful not to make a sound, I start to glide through the water, Gregor's scary theme song playing in my head.

DERRRRRRR-DUN! DERRRRRR-DUN! DER-DUN! DER-DUN! DER-DUN! DER-DUN!

But just as I get to the desk, disaster strikes. My tail gets caught in a strand from my seaweed blanket. I try to tug it free but end up getting even more tangled. I pull as hard as I can. The balled-up blanket sails through the water, hits the shelf above my bed, and sends my finball trophy flying.

"Eh? Uh! Wass going on?" Lenny says sleepily as I try to untangle myself from the seaweed.

Hmm, not exactly the kind of surprise

attack I'd been planning. But the problem is, my room's way too small. You can't really sneak up on something when it's really close to begin with. You need a little distance from the target to be able to plan your attack. I decide to investigate the rest of the house to see what I can find.

But as I swim through my bedroom door, I hear a really horrible noise. It's like a crab grinding glass with its pincers. Or a ship's foghorn that has a seagull stuck inside it. It can only be one thing—my mom, singing while she makes breakfast. I start to grin. When

Mom is singing, she goes off into her own little world and doesn't notice a thing. She will make the perfect target. Let the ambushing begin!

While Mom keeps screeching like a harpooned mermaid, I get to the kitchen door without being seen. Then I poke one side of my hammerhead through the door and swivel my eye around, trying to spot my prey. There she is, at the far end of the kitchen, putting breakfast things on a tray, still singing away. Now that I'm closer I can actually make out some of the words in between the screeches:

"*Like an anchor—dropped for the very first time. Like an a-a-a-anchor . . .*"

Oh, please!

I slink my way into the room and slide behind the giant glass vase of flower fish in the corner. Honestly, I don't know why we can't just have regular sea flowers like everyone else. It was my

COVE SWEET COVE

dad's idea of a joke. But the trouble is, my dad's idea of a joke isn't ever anybody else's idea of a joke. I don't know how he managed to get elected as the new Shark Point mayor.

I get myself ready to pounce. *This must be how Gregor feels before a fight,* I think as my heart starts to pound.

I hear my unsuspecting prey swimming for the door, her apron strings swishing in the water behind her. Closer and closer she comes.

"Made of iron, shiny and fine," she wails.

I tense my muscles. Closer she comes. I arch my back. And closer. I get ready to pounce. Closer. NOW!

CHAPTER 2

Okay, I'll admit it, the ambush didn't go 100 percent according to plan. It went about 10 percent according to plan. The surprise part worked great—that was the 10 percent—but what happened right after wasn't so good. The chain of events went like this:

1. I leaped out from behind the flower fish, yelling at the top of my lungs . . .

2. Mom screeched—and this time she wasn't singing . . .

3. Mom dropped the breakfast tray . . .

4. I smashed into it . . .

5. And sent everything flying EVERYWHERE.

And now everything has gone dark on one side of the room. I swivel my right eye but can't see anything out of it. My ambush has turned into a terrible tragedy!

"I'm blind! I'm blind!" I cry.

Mom stops screaming. "Breakfast bowl," she gasps, pointing a shaking fin at me.

I blink my working eye at her in disbelief. Why is she calling me breakfast bowl? Has my ambush made her go crazy? And why isn't she looking more concerned? Her only son has just told her he can't see anymore! From one eye, at least.

"What?" I say.

"Breakfast bowl."

"Why do you keep calling me that?" I yell. "I've gone blind in one eye."

"It's a breakfast bowl," she squeals.

"What are you talking about?" I start to panic. I have gone blind and my mom has gone crazy. So far this is not turning out to be a very good morning.

"You've got a breakfast bowl over your eye," Mom explains.

I shake my head and, sure enough, a bowl falls off and drifts to the floor, leaving Kelp Krispies trickling down my face. Although I'm relieved I'm not actually blind and my mom isn't actually crazy, I can't help thinking sadly that this would never, ever happen to Gregor the Gnasher.

"What in the name of all the oceans were you doing, Harry?" Mom asks.

"Sorry, Mom," I reply, looking at the floor. "I was only trying to ambush you."

"Only trying to ambush me!" Mom echoes, wiping the Kelp Krispies off my head with the bottom of her apron. (I bet that's never happened to Gregor either!) "Hammerheads don't ambush things, you silly little starfish!"

I cringe with embarrassment. How

am I ever going to be taken as seriously as a great white when my mom calls me names like that? "I was trying to be like Gregor the Gnasher," I try to explain.

Mom sighs. "I'll never understand why you kids think that tooth-head is some kind of hero."

"Hero? Did someone say hero?" my dad booms, entering the kitchen. "Well, here I am! Ha, ha, ha!"

I told you his jokes weren't funny.

"Oh, you'll always be our hero, darling," laughs Mom, before giving him a massive kiss.

I think I might be sick. There's only so much a ten-year-old hammerhead can take in one morning.

"What was all that noise about?" Dad asks. He looks around at the mess. "And why's my breakfast on the floor?"

To stop Mom from going through the whole ambush disaster again, I decide to change the conversation.

"How's the speech going, Dad?"

My dad's working on his first ever speech as mayor. Most of Shark Point will be there to hear it, so I hope he doesn't tell any jokes.

"It's going great," Dad replies, "but I think I should start with a joke. Better yet, maybe two jokes. . . . "

Where's a fisherman's hook when you need one?

"How about this one?" says Dad as Mom starts picking up the plates and bowls from the floor. "What do you call a fish with no eyes?"

I stare at him and shake my head. "I dunno."

"A fsh!" he replies, before roaring with laughter. "Get it? No *i*'s. Ha ha ha!"

He sees me staring at him, not laughing. "Okay, well, maybe I'll think of a different joke. I'll be in the living room." And with that, he turns and swims back down the hall.

"Honey, can you turn on your hammer-
-vision and see if you can find the lid
for the teapot while I clean up?" Mom
asks. "I must have dropped it in your . . .
ambush."

I turn on the special sensors in my head
and start swimming around the kitchen.
Having sensors is like having a bunch
of extra eyes that can see inside and
through things. And because our heads
are so big, hammerheads have the most
powerful sensors in the entire ocean. It's
pretty cool. Especially if you want to find
out where your parents have hidden your
Christmas presents. Mom goes crazy

when I do this. She says the reason we have sensors is so that we can find food even if it's buried deep beneath the sea-bed. She says that using our sensors to find hidden presents is wrong. But then, she would say that—she's a parent. As far as parents are concerned, everything that's fun is "wrong"!

I find the teapot lid right away—behind a sea cucumber on the table.

"Thank you, dear," Mom says as I give it to her. "You've certainly got excellent hammer-vision—and it's so much more useful than ambushing. I mean, who needs to hunt for prey these days, when you can just go to the supermarket?"

"But ambushing's exciting and cool," I reply. "When I use my sensors, I'm just . . . trying to find stuff."

"What is cool," says Mom, "is your class outing to the *Titan* today. So you'd better get some breakfast inside you or you're going to be late."

The *Titan*! I'd completely forgotten about the school trip to the shipwreck. It wasn't as exciting as going out to the deep ocean to see great whites—but it was a day out of school.

I barely manage to cram down some breakfast before I hear Ralph shouting for me outside. Ralph is a pilot fish and one of my best friends.

I grab my backpack and head for the door.

"Bye, Mom. Bye, Dad."

"Bye, angelfish!" Mom calls.

"Bye, son," Dad hollers. "What kind of fish feels the most pain?"

I pretend not to hear him.

"A sore-dine! Ha, ha, ha!"

My parents are so embarrassing!

Outside, Ralph is swimming around our front yard, his silver stripes glinting in the sunshine.

"Hey, Harry, all ready for the school trip?" he says as soon as he sees me.

"You bet," I reply.

"So what did you have for breakfast today?" he asks.

"Shrimp Pop-Tarts."

"Cool, my favorite. Okay then, open wide, I'm going in!"

I open my mouth as wide as I can and Ralph dives in and starts nibbling at my teeth.

This is what pilot fish do, by the way—they eat the scraps of food from between sharks' teeth. They're kind of like swimming, talking toothbrushes.

As soon as Ralph has finished we start making our way toward the center of town.

We've just reached the water park when Joe shows up. Joe is a bright yellow jellyfish and another one of my friends. One of the coolest things about Joe is that he has a bunch of arms. Well, a *lot* of arms. The only uncool thing about Joe's arms is that it can take a *long* time to high-fin. I like him a lot, but he can be a worrier.

"Good morning, Joe," I say.

"Is it?" Joe replies.

Ralph and I stare at him.

"Of course it is—we're going on the trip to the *Titan*," says Ralph.

"Aren't you looking forward to it?" I ask.

"Not really," says Joe. "I'll probably get my tentacles trapped in a porthole, or be harpooned by a diver. Or lose my packed lunch in the wreckage, or—"

"Okay, okay, we get the point," says Ralph.

Joe's yellow tentacles quiver. "Why can't we just stay in school? It's much safer."

"Oh, come on, Joe," I say. "It'll be good to see more of the ocean."

"Why?" he replies. "It's all the same—just a lot of wet."

You can't really argue with that, so we stop at the stores and look in Seahorse Sports and Leisure to check out the latest games. Then we make our way to school. My heart sinks as I see Rick Reef and Donny Dogfish by the gates. Rick is

a blacktip reef shark, which means he has this really cool black tip on his dorsal fin. He is wearing his matching black leather jacket (as usual) and showing off (as usual) by swimming really quickly through all the groups of kids. Donny is cheering him on (as usual), doing a sports commentary as Rick speeds around.

"And Rick Reef takes a sharp right past some second-grade clown fish and a left through a group of first-grade dolphins. See them scatter as the swimming captain speeds down the lane."

Rick is the school swimming captain and loves to let everyone know it.

Suddenly Rick spots our group and swims straight for us, pulling up at the last minute and showering us with air bubbles.

"Well, if it isn't old Anchor Face," he says.

"Good one, Rick," says Donny, smirking away beside him.

"Oh, grow up, Rick," says Ralph.

"Be quiet, Toothpick," says Rick. Then he turns to Joe. "Oh look, it's Jelly Belly."

Donny is almost dying laughing, but before anyone can say anything else, the school bell rings.

"Last one in's a sea snail," shouts Rick as he swims for the door.

I'll show him who's a sea snail, I think as I charge after him.

"What are you doing?" Ralph cries.

"Be careful," Joe calls. "You might sprain your tail or pull a fin muscle."

But I don't care. Nothing and no one is going to stop me. I'm going to teach that reef shark show-off a lesson. He might be the fastest swimmer in the school, but I have surprise on my side. Rick thinks no one would actually bother racing him because he's the swimming captain, so he isn't going that fast. I zoom past him into the school.

I speed along the corridor. The

classroom door is getting closer and closer. I swivel my left eye backward and see that Rick's gaining on me.

DERRRRRRR-DUN! DERRRRRRR-DUN! DER-DUN! DER-DUN! DER-DUN! DER-DUN!

I think of Gregor the Gnasher's theme song and make a desperate lunge for the door.

DERRRRRRR-DUN! DERRRRRRR-DUN! DER

"Ow!"

I'm so busy keeping one eye on Rick, I forget that the doorway is kind of narrow and go slamming straight into it. I desperately flail my tail, but it's no good. I'm stuck—my humongous hammerhead wedged in the door.

"Hey, Harry," I hear Rick tease from behind me, chuckling, "I've heard of getting something in your eye—but a whole door frame?"

The entire class starts laughing their heads off. And they are still laughing as Ralph and Joe help me unwedge myself. I've never felt more embarrassed as I slink over to my desk.

But it had felt so good when I was actually beating Rick in the race. I decide

then and there that I don't care what it takes, I'm going to prove I'm just as good as the rest of them. I'm going to show them all what a hammerhead can do!

CHAPTER 3

Creeeeeeeeeeeeeeeeaaaaaaaaaak!!!

At first I think the noise is coming from the rotting planks of the *Titan*. *Creeeeeeeeeeeee-ak-ak-ak-ak-ak!!!*

But it isn't the *Titan*.

It's Joe's backside.

Ralph and I give him a look.

"Well, it is a bit scary!" Joe says, turning from bright yellow to bright pink with embarrassment.

And to be honest, Joe is right. It *is* scary.

As Mrs. Shelby, our sea-turtle teacher, leads us closer to the *Titan*, the butter-flies start to flap in my tummy too. The

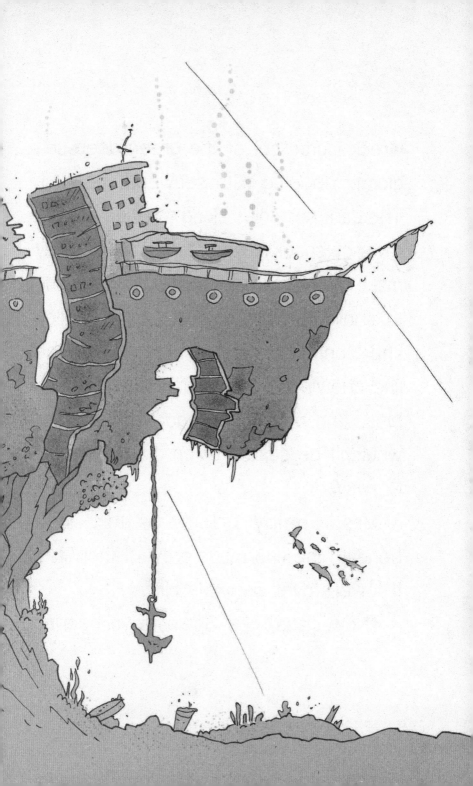

wreck looms out of the green deep-sea gloom, dripping with seaweed and rust. The dark portholes along the side are like rows of spooky eyes staring at us. They make me want to shiver. But I'm not going to show that I'm scared, not with Rick and Donny hanging at the back of the line chewing sea gum and blowing bubbles. And besides, Gregor the Gnasher wouldn't be scared of an old shipwreck. No way.

Mrs. Shelby brings us to a halt beneath the enormous prow of the *Titan*. It towers over us like a cliff.

"Now, class," Mrs. Shelby says, peering

over her little round glasses. The shadow from the shipwreck has made her face dark. "Under no circumstances are you to go into the wreck. It is very, very dangerous in there. The *Titan* has been on the seabed for over a hundred years, and is rusting and rotting away. It could collapse at any moment and turn you into fish paste!"

Everyone giggles, until we see the serious look on Mrs. Shelby's face.

"I mean it. You're here to look at the area around the *Titan* for your geography project." Mrs. Shelby begins handing out round, flat pieces of rock with writing. "Here is a

list of everything I want you to find."

Now, normally I love lists, but not this one.

1. A barnacle—boring!
2. Three different types of shell—more boring!
3. At least three colors of seaweed—I'm seriously starting to fall asleep now.
4. Zzzzzzzzzzzzzzzzzzzzzzzz—see?

Ralph fins me in the side to wake me up.

"Once you've found everything on your checklist, meet back here, under the prow, okay?" Mrs. Shelby calls.

We all nod and start to swish away.

"Wait!"

We all stop.

"I need to put you in your groups."

Mrs. Shelby has a thing about us working in groups. It's really annoying. Doesn't she realize that I'm a shark, a lone hunter of the waves? I bet Gregor never gets put in a group. When she first starts reading the names of my group, it isn't too bad.

1. Me.
2. Joe—Yay!
3. Ralph—Double yay!
4. Donny—Boooooo!
5. Rick—Double boooooo! with extra boooooo! on the side and sprinkled with grated boooooo!

"Now, don't forget what I told you," Mrs. Shelby yells as we start to swim off. "No going inside the *Titan*—UNDER ANY CIRCUMSTANCES!"

"Yes, Mrs. Shelby," we all mutter.

Of course Rick immediately takes the lead in our group and decides which way we swim. We all follow him around to the collapsed stern of the *Titan*. It must have hit the seabed with a massive crunch. The whole back of the ship with its enormous propeller is ripped open and we can see right inside. The decks are layered like Mom's coral cake, and great piles of stuff like bed frames and chairs and doors and ladders have all fallen out onto the seabed in a big fan-shaped mess. It's starting to get covered in seaweed and barnacles and coral—it won't be long before the whole thing turns into a new reef. And Rick is leading us straight into it!

I look around but can only see the back of Mrs. Shelby's shell as she comforts Penny Puffer-Fish. Penny has gotten all spiky. Puffer fish only get spiky when they are very afraid and think they are about to die. Penny must be *very* scared of the *Titan*.

"Rick!" I call as loudly as I dare. "You heard what Mrs. Shelby said."

Rick looks back, smirks, and says, "I thought you were a hammerhead, not a scaredy-catfish. Donny and I are going into the wreck, 'cause that's where all the best barnacles are, and we're going to have the best project. Are you coming, or are you going to stay there making bubbles with your rears?"

Donny and Rick slap fins and swoosh off, right toward the hole in the back of the *Titan*.

Well, I'm not going to stand for that. "Come on, guys, let's go!" I cry.

"Where?" Ralph and Joe say together.

"With them!" I shout, pointing after Rick and Donny. I can see that Ralph isn't sure, and Joe is actually trying to hide under himself.

"It'll be fine," I say.

"Yeah, if 'FINE' stands for 'we'll be Fish food, If Not Exterminated,'" Joe mutters from beneath his tentacles.

With a bit of pushing and pulling, Ralph and I and, finally, Joe, head off toward the wreck.

Rick and Donny have already disappeared by the time we get to the massive hole in the back of the ship. Jagged strips of metal hang above us as sharp as razor shells. Thick, waterlogged beams of wood ripped from floors and walls look splintery and deadly.

"It feels colder. Does it feel colder to you?" Joe says with a shiver. "I'm turning from a jellyfish into an ice pop. I'm going to freeze and die. I've already lost the feeling in my seventh tentacle!"

Ralph swims up to me with a barnacle in his fins. "Got one—let's go," he says with a tremble in his voice.

I'm just about to agree when some stuff happens. Stuff that means I'm not leaving the wreck. Well, not yet.

The stuff that happens is:

1. Rick appears with
a big, toothy grin.

2. Donny arrives too
(but he doesn't look as grinny.

In fact, he looks a bit sick to his stomach).

3. Rick flubbers the side of my hammer
with his fin.

4. **Flubbering** the side of my hammer with his fin makes my stupid rubbery head **boing** about and makes my words come out all **flibbery**.

5. "D-d-d-d-d-d-don't d-d-d-d-d-d-d-do d-d-d-d-d-d-dat!"

See?

Luckily, Ralph and Joe know what to do. They each catch an end of my head and hold on tightly until it stops *flibber-flabbering*.

"Come on, Rubberhead," Rick says, "look what we've found!"

I hate it when Rick flubbers my head.

Hammerheads are the only sharks you can do it to, and he does it all the time. It makes me feel dorkey. Well, I'm not going to let him see me scared, too!

With one kick of my tail, I follow, and since Ralph and Joe are still holding on to my head, they come too.

As I swim on into the *Titan* it gets darker and darker. I'm not really noticing what's around me—I'm just determined to keep up with Rick and Donny. I can hear Ralph and Joe making muffled cries as they hug my head, but I'm not stopping for anything.

Then!

Wow!

We have come out into a huge ball-room right in the middle of the *Titan*. The whole place is lit up, but I don't understand why. Then I look up to the ceiling. There's a hole in it and sunlight from the ocean surface is pouring in. I can see more collapsed decks above it leading

up to massive smokestacks, bent over at crazy angles. They look like they've been caught in mid-fall by invisible hands. It looks really spooky! Although the middle of the ballroom is quite bright from the sun, the edges are covered in really dark shadow. Anything could be hiding there, waiting to pounce. . . .

Rick starts swimming around the ballroom, darting in and out of the seaweed-covered pillars. Then he starts doing barrel rolls and fin slides. He tail-flips into a double nosey and skims underneath me with a triple gill slap.

Show-off, I think.

"How cool is this place, and how cool am I?" shouts Rick as he shoots off again.

That's the final straw. It's time I show this show-off exactly what a hammer-head is capable of! Shaking Ralph and Joe clear, I speed off after Rick, knocking Donny right out of the way as I do.

Rick skids into a full tailspin. I give him

my best double gill flip. Rick just laughs in my face and is off again, tail-grinding along a handrail and single-finning across the hole between two torn-open rooms.

I follow. And then I make several mistakes, so many I can make a list of them.

1. I follow Rick without thinking—bad.

2. Not thinking means I don't measure the hole he goes through—bad, bad.

3. Not measuring the hole he goes through means I crash into the ragged gap in a half-twisty double-fin with pike—bad, bad, bad.

4. And I was probably traveling at twice my normal speed—bad beyond belief.

Creeeeeeeeeaaaaaaaaaaaakkkk!!!!

"That wasn't my rear!" I hear Joe shouting as I thud into the wall with a huge . . . thud.

I have just enough time to look up before the half-collapsed smokestacks above the ballroom start falling toward us with a horrible crashing, smashing, tearing, ripping sound.

And then everything goes dark!

CHAPTER 4

I think what happens next is this:

1. Donny crashes into Rick.

2. Rick crashes into me.

3. I crash into Joe.

4. Two of Joe's tentacles get stuck in my nostrils and I have to shake my head like crazy until my slimy jellyfish friend lets go.

69

The smokestack has crashed down over the hole in the ballroom ceiling, and nearly all the light is gone. I try to keep calm, but it's not easy. Especially when you've had jellyfish fingers stuck up your nose. But now that Joe has finally let go, I'm finding it easier to breathe. And I might not be able to see much, but I can still *hear* stuff.

I can hear someone's teeth chattering.

"Is everyone okay?" I ask.

"I want my mommy," says Joe.

"Me too!" says Donny.

"M-m-m-e-e thr-r-e-e-e," says someone else.

"Ralph? Is that you?" I ask.

"N-n-n-n-no," says Rick, "It-it-it-it's me."

I'm shocked. Big, brave Rick the reef shark is so scared he can't keep his teeth still!

"Wh-wh-wh-what happened?" Rick asks.

"The smokestack fell down," I say.

"We need to get out of here!" yells Donny. "It's not safe! We'll be crushed!"

"He's r-r-r-r-right!" Rick says.

"Wait!" I start to say, but Donny is off. I feel him skim past me.

"No!" Donny calls back. "I'm going back out the way we—"

BOINNNNNNNNNNNG . . .

CREEEEEEEEEEEEEEEEEEEEEEEEAK . . .

CRASH!

I think these noises are:

1. Donny going *BOINNNNNNNNNNNG* as he bounces off a big metal door that has blocked the way we came in.
2. The vibration of the *BOINNNNNNNNNNNG* causing the smokestack to *CREEEEEEEEEEEEEEEEAK* again.
3. The *CREEEEEEEEEEEEEEEEEEEEEEEAK* of the smokestack causing a load of wood from the ceiling to *CRASH* down. Only just missing me, Joe, and Rick!

"Nobody move!" I shout. "We can't see anything, and every time we knock into something we make things even worse."

"Wh-wh-wh-wh-why are y-y-y-y-you s-s-s-suddenly in ch-ch-ch-ch-charge?" Rick chatters.

"Because my mouth isn't doing weird things with my teeth," I say.

"I-I-I-I-I-I'm j-j-j-just c-c-c-c-cold," Rick whines. "That's all."

Yeah right, I think. But I don't say anything, because I have more important things to think about. Like where's Ralph?

"Where's Ralph?" I ask.

Silence.

"Ralph! Ralph!" I shout.

"He's probably dead," Joe says gloomily.

"I told you we'd be fish food if we came in here."

Silence.

POP.

"Joe!" Donny yells.

"Sorry," Joe mutters.

I swim around a bit, slowly and carefully. "Ralph? Are you okay?" But there's no sound apart from—

CREEEEEEEEEEEEEEEEEAK.

The wood and the smokestack shift again. But this time with no one bumping into anything. This is getting

serious. We're trapped in a collapsing ship and I can't find my best friend! I clamp my jaw shut to stop *my* teeth from chattering with fear. I have to at least pretend to be brave or we'll never make it out.

"Okay, listen up, everyone, we've got to find Ralph and then we can get out of here."

"He's your f-f-f-friend, you f-f-f-find him!" says Rick. Donny just looks away.

I'm not going to get any help from the Terrified Twins, that's for sure.

I turn to look at Joe. He's wobbling his tentacles around in panic, mumbling,

"Fish food, If Not Exterminated. Why doesn't anyone ever listen to me?"

I'm beginning to wish I *had* listened to him.

There's nothing else I can do. I gulp and try not to look scared. "Right, you all stay here and I'll go and look for Ralph."

I kick my tail and swim off cautiously. My goggly eyes are a bit more used to the dark now, and I can start to make out some shapes. Lots of the ballroom's ceiling has come down all around us, but the huge rusty smokestack is lying right across the hole. You couldn't even fit a flatfish through the gap now. We are really, truly trapped.

I start to swim around in a circle, looking up and down, hoping that Ralph hasn't been hit by any of the falling wood. My heart is beating so hard I can feel it shaking my whole body.

From the other side of the ballroom Joe starts muttering again. "I reckon we're going to be stuck here so long we won't be home for dinner."

I swim alongside a pile of crushed chairs.

"In fact, we'll probably freeze to death before we ever get out."

I dart over broken, seaweed-covered tables.

"The only way I'm getting out of here is if some whale crashes his way in and wants a jellyfish ice pop."

I stick my head into a slimy fireplace. Still no Ralph.

"Or we'll get crushed up into plankton and eaten. Everyone will wonder where we've gone. They'll probably run a missing fish ad in the *Seaweed Times*, but it'll be too late. I just know we're not going to get out! I can sense it."

I'm just about to tell Joe to shut up, when something hits me like a wet fish in the face.

Sense it!

Joe said he could *sense* it.

Oh flibbery-flump! Of course. I can use my sensors to try to find Ralph. I quickly turn them on and start moving my hammerhead about, scanning the room. It's really faint, but I can definitely sense some movement coming from the other end of the ballroom. I swim off past Joe and I zoom in on the tiny vibration I can sense in my hammer.

BRRRRRMMMMMM.

As I reach the far end of the ballroom the vibration gets much stronger. It's not clear exactly where the vibration is coming from, but it's definitely around here somewhere.

I look left.

BRRRRrrrrrrrrmmmmmmmm . . .

I look right.

. . . mmmmMMMMBBBBRRRRRR!!!

I go right, and find a big wooden pillar. Underneath the pillar is a grand piano—one of those that has a big lid on top. It's standing all lopsided on broken legs. The lid is shut, and covered in pieces of the fallen ceiling. But what I see sticking out from the lid makes my hammerhead quiver. Waving slowly in the tiny opening is the bottom half of Ralph.

He's trapped inside the piano!

"Ralph! Ralph! It's me!" I shout.

"Harry?" Ralph squeaks from inside the piano. "Help! I can't move."

I rush forward and try to push the piano lid up with my fin.

It won't budge.

I flip around and shove my tail up against the wooden pillar that's on top. I push as hard as I can.

It won't budge either.

"Or maybe we'll get captured by leggy air-breathers who are doing research on the shipwreck, and no one will ever see us again," I hear Joe muttering from the other side of the room.

I take three swishes of my tail back-ward, turn and face the piano head-on, and leap toward it hammer-first. It hurts, but I manage to get the flat edge of my head into the opening beneath the piano lid.

I flick my tail harder and the lid creaks up a tiny bit, giving me enough room to slide my eye into the crack. I can see Ralph. He's on his side and still stuck, but he looks okay.

"Don't worry, Ralph," I say. "I'll have you out of here soon."

I can feel the weight of the pillar on the piano lid pressing onto my head,

but I don't care. I've got to get Ralph out. But how? Maybe if I twisted my head sideways I'd be able to lift the lid higher.

I start kicking really hard with my tail fin.

The lid moves up a little.

I kick harder.

It moves up a little more.

I flap and flip my tail as hard as I can and twist my head until—

The lid springs up, tumbling the pillar onto the floor.

Ralph speeds out of the piano faster than a sailfish. I'm right behind him.

"Yaaaaaaaaaaaaaaaaaaaaaaaaaaaaaaaay!"
we both scream, high-finning each other
and bumping chests.

"I thought I was never going to get
out of there," Ralph gasps. "What happened?"

"Part of the ceiling caved in," I explain

as we swim back over to the others. "And a smokestack came down and blocked the hole."

We swim over to Joe, who is still sittting on the floor, hiding behind his tentacles.

"Look—I found Ralph!" I say.

Joe moves one of his tentacles and peeps out. But when he sees Ralph, he doesn't look happy.

"What's wrong?" I say.

"We're still doomed. Even if nothing happens to us, we'll still starve to death." Joe puts his tentacle back over his eyes.

Ralph and I roll *our* eyes. I look about and my heart sinks. "Where are Rick and Donny?"

"They said they weren't waiting for you to find Ralph and were going to smash their way out," Joe says.

CRAAAAAAAAAAAAAAAAASH!!!!

"That must be them, then," says Joe.

Oh no!

I swim as fast as I can to the metal door. Rick and Donny are bashing themselves against it in a panic. I try to swim between Rick and the door. "Stop it!" I yell. "You'll bring the whole ship down on us!"

But Donny noses me out of the way

and Rick thuds into the door again.

There's nothing I can do to stop them.

"Look at the smokestack!" Ralph yells.

I look up. The smokestack is shifting again and the planks holding it up are beginning to give way. If we don't get out of here soon, we're fish cakes.

I dart back to Ralph and Joe. "Come on, let's try over there!" I point a fin to the far corner of the ballroom. Then I call back to Rick and Donny. "Come on, you two."

"You go if you w-w-w-want to!" Rick shouts at me. "But we're not moving. This is the way w-w-w-w-we came in,

and this is the way we're going out. That way will just take you farther into the ship, and you'll be even more trapped."

I don't want to leave them, but if there's another way out I *have* to find it.

Joe, Ralph, and I swim along the wall, until we reach a jumbled pile of rotting furniture. We swim higher and higher up the pile, until, right at the top, we find a big sofa with springs popping out all over it, like a spiky puffer fish.

"Careful," I say to the other two as I dodge the springs. Once we've gotten past the pyramid of furniture, I can't believe my goggly eyes. There's a door!

And it doesn't seem to be blocked by anything. "Let's see where it goes," I call to the other two. "If it leads out of the ship, we can go and get Donny and Rick."

It's even colder on the other side of the doorway. We swim down a short, dark corridor, which opens onto a massive landing and a huge broken staircase as wide as a whale sandwich.

"Wow," I say.

Huge marble pillars have toppled down and smashed through the staircase. They look like a giant's fingers breaking through the wood.

Ralph and Joe start swimming around,
looking for a way out, but there is only
the staircase, which just seems to lead
up to nowhere.

"Looks like we're stuck," says Ralph.

"Trapped in a watery grave," says Joe mournfully.

I swim to the bottom of the stairs and squint through the waving strands of seaweed and murky water. Then I catch sight of something.

"Yes!" I cry.

Up high, almost but not quite out of range of my hammerhead eyes, I can see a tiny glimmer of light. I swivel my eyes and focus them as hard as I can. There, high above us, in the roof of the *Titan*, is a skylight. It's been smashed, and through it I can see a beam of sunlight in the water.

It's a way out!

We're saved!

Or we would have been. But that's when the whole ship begins to shake and rumble, and the hugest *CRASH!!!* yet comes from the direction of the ballroom.

CHAPTER 5

Ralph, Joe, and I burst back into the ballroom and find the water churning up like a whirlpool, full of dust and bits of wood.

"Rick!" I call. "Donny! Are you okay?" But there's no answer. "Split up," I say to Ralph and Joe. "We've got to find them and get up those stairs."

"Okay," Ralph says.

Joe is fishing pieces of dirt out of his mouth with his tentacles. "Mmmph mmmph we'll be exploded into jelly beans mmmph," he says.

"Come on!" I say.

We all swim off in different direc- tions. I head for the metal door, and just when I think the day can't get any worse, it does.

Donny is swimming in circles by the door, crying and shaking.

"Where's Rick?" I say.

Donny slowly points a trembling fin behind me.

I turn and squint through the murky water. And see Rick trapped inside a glittery gold cage. I can hardly believe my eyes. So I blink them. Then I swivel them. But I wasn't seeing things—Rick really is trapped inside a glittery gold cage.

What I think happened is this:

1. Donny and Rick kept smashing into the door. **(NOT GOOD.)**

2. The vibrations they caused traveled up through the ship until they reached the ceiling. **(NOT GOODER.)**

3. This shook one of the enormous chandeliers so much that it crashed down on top of Rick and trapped him on the floor. **(NOT GOODER-ER!)**

"Get me out," Rick wails.

RUUUUUUUUUUMMMMMBLE!

The whole ship vibrates. Clouds of splinters puff out from the beams above

us like coral blooms. The ballroom is about to collapse completely. Ralph and Joe swim over in a panic.

"Don't just float there! Get me out!" Rick yells.

Donny is still swimming around and around in circles. I grab him by the fins. "Donny! We need your help. We won't be able to get Rick out on our own."

Donny's eyes are filled with tears, and his bottom lip is trembling. "You don't even like Rick, so why would you want to help him?"

"Well, I wouldn't leave him here to get crushed, would I?"

Donny sniffs. "I guess not."

"Good, now are you going to help us or what?"

Donny nods, and I pat him on the fin.

"Get me out!" Rick screams.

"Right," I say, trying to sound like I know what I'm doing and I have a plan, which I don't. "Ummmm . . ."

The chandelier is massive. The gold rails are all bent over in arches. There are lots of little rings attached, which were probably used for glass jewels or something, but now they're just empty. These rings are what I'm *really* interested in.

Now I have a plan!

"Okay, everyone wedge your fin into a ring on this side of the chandelier," I say.

No one moves.

Joe opens his mouth to speak, but I cut him off.

"No, we're not going to freeze to death, or become ice pops and eaten by whales, or get turned into plankton, or get featured in the *Seaweed Times*,

101

or get captured by leggy air-breathers, or starve to death, or explode into jelly beans. At least, we won't if you *hurry up!*" I say.

"No, it's not that," Joe says.

"What is it, then?" I ask.

"GET ME OUT!" Rick yells.

"What if you don't have a fin?" Joe asks.

"Oh! Well, use your strongest tentacles," I say.

RUUUUUUUUUUMMMMMBLE!

"Now!" I shout. "We don't have time to be scared!"

I wriggle my right fin up into a ring and shove my dorsal fin against it. The others do the same, but I can see the fear in their faces as they all look over at me to show that they're ready.

This had better work.

"Rick—get ready to swim out, okay?" I say.

"Just hurry up!" Rick yells.

"Okay, everyone!" I shout. "Swim up now!"

I kick with my tail. Ralph and Donny do the same. Joe does something complicated with his tentacles.

The chandelier shifts a tiny bit, but not enough!

"Get me out!"

CRRRRREEEEEEEEAAAAAKKKKKK!!!

This is our last chance!

"One . . . ," I count.

"Two . . ."

Joe's bottom toots.

"Three!"

I kick and kick and kick my tail, harder than I ever have before.

The chandelier starts to move.

"Keep going!" I shout.

Kick.

Kick.

Kick. Kick. Kick!

The chandelier lurches upward. Rick flattens himself against the floor and slides

underneath the edges of the cage. He's
out!

"Okay, let go!" I yell.

We all swim away and the chandelier
crashes back to the floor.

"Follow me," I say, swimming for the doorway leading to the staircase. We zoom across the deck, up over the pile of wrecked furniture, past the springs of the busted sofa, and out through the door into the dark corridor. I can hear the others flapping behind me. I turn to make sure everyone is through the door okay. Rick, Donny, Ralph, and then Joe, puffing up behind. Jellyfish aren't exactly built for speed, but he's doing a great job.

"Everyone up the stairs. Up to the skylight. Come on!"

We race up the stairs toward the skylight

and burst out of the roof like corks from a bottle, whooping and high-finning each other like crazy. Down below us there is a final *RUUUUUUUUUUMMMMMMBLE* as the *Titan* collapses like a seashell being squashed by a giant fin!

CHAPTER 6

I don't think I've ever seen Mrs. Shelby look so happy. She's smiling wide enough to swallow a baby whale.

"Harry! Ralph! Joe! Donny! Rick!" she calls to us. "Oh my goodness, I've been so worried!"

We swim down to the seabed, where

Mrs. Shelby has gathered the class together out of danger. All the kids look pretty scared of the noises coming from the *Titan*. Not only is Penny Puffer-Fish still spiky, but all the hermit-crab kids have gone right inside their shells and shut the doors.

We skid to a halt in front of the class, me doing a triple nosey and the best gill grind ever.

"We thought you were trapped inside!" Mrs. Shelby says, hugging each of us. She probably hugs Joe just a little bit too tight, because he toots again, but she doesn't seem to mind.

I'm just about to tell her everything
that happened, when a fin slaps onto
my face and covers my mouth so I
can't speak. The fin belongs to Rick.
He pushes in front of me. "Well, Mrs.
Shelby, if I hadn't gotten everyone out,

we might not have made it at all. Right, Donny?"

I stare so hard at Rick that it feels like my eyes might pop out of my hammerhead. I can't believe what he's saying. Just a couple of minutes ago he was shrieking for help, stuck under a chandelier.

"I tried to tell them not to go into the *Titan*, Mrs. Shelby, but they wouldn't listen," Rick continues. "And I couldn't just

let them go in alone, could I?"

I glance at Ralph and Joe. They look just as annoyed as I am. We're all so annoyed, we can't get any words out!

This is so unfair. I start to open my mouth to complain, but then all the kids in the class start laughing. Great! So now not only do they think I've got a weird hammerhead, they think I'm reckless, too. But as I swivel my eyes around I notice that the rest of the class is all pointing and laughing at Rick. As he swims around in front of Mrs. Shelby I see something glinting and sparkling on his back. Some jewels from the chandelier have gotten

caught on his
dorsal fin like
a princess's
tiara.

He looks
ridiculous.

I begin laughing
too, so hard I end
up doing three barrel
rolls. By the time I finish, Mrs. Shelby is
waving her big flippers to calm the class
down and Rick is just floating there with a
bright red face.

"What are you all laughing at?" he
whines.

Ha! Now that he knows what it feels like, maybe he won't flubber my head so much in the future. Win!

Ralph swims past me and turns to the class. "We wouldn't have gotten out of there if it wasn't for Harry, Mrs. Shelby," he says. "It was Rick who wanted to go into the *Titan*, not Harry. When the smokestack collapsed and everything went dark, I got trapped inside a piano and it was Harry and his hammerhead sensors that got me out. Rick was too busy trying to save his own skin. Harry is the bravest shark in the whole sea."

I feel my hammerhead turning coral

pink as the whole class looks from Rick's tiara to me. I don't really like being the center of attention—even if it's for a good thing. But Ralph keeps going. "And when Rick got trapped under a chandelier, it was Harry who showed us how to get him out, and it was Harry's awesome hammerhead eyes that found the way out through the skylight. All Rick did while we were in there was show off and cry."

Everyone in the class is staring open-mouthed at me. Even Mrs. Shelby. I don't know what to say.

Mrs. Shelby closes her mouth, thinks

for a moment, then calls Rick and me forward. "You two boys are very, very naughty for disobeying me and going into the *Titan*. If you'd listened to me, none of this would have happened, and none of you would have been in any danger at all. Do you understand?"

We both nod. This makes Rick's tiara sparkle, and the three angelfish behind us giggle under their breath.

"Really, I should punish you all for going into the ship," Mrs. Shelby continues, "but since Harry has been so brave, and he managed to bring you all back to safety, I'll let you off the hook.

But just this once, understand?"

The class cheers and claps. Ralph and Joe swim up to me and we high-fin and high-tentacle.

Donny swims off to one side with Rick, and I watch as he whispers in his ear, telling him about the tiara. Rick twists and turns his pointy face, trying to get a look at his fin.

"Get it off me!" he yells at Donny.

Donny pulls at the jewels with his teeth and Rick twists some more. But the jewels are stuck tight and the sharks' struggles only make the class laugh even louder. Donny and Rick look like they are dancing together in that really embarrassing way that moms and dads do.

Mrs. Shelby calms the class down all over again. Then we set off back to school. As we go I make my final list of the day—of all the good things that have happened:

1. Everyone is safe. *(Genius.)*

2. Rick's tiara incident is going to keep him from

me for a while. *(Super genius!)*

out as the worst day ever has turned

ay ever! *(More-super-than-Rick's-*

a hammerhead might not be so

all. . . .

THE END

picking on me for a while. *(Super genius!)*

3. What started out as the worst day ever has turned into the best day ever! *(More-super-than-Rick's-tiara genius!)*

Being a hammerhead might not be so bad after all. . . .

THE END

Lights! Camera! Hammerhead!

CHAPTER 1

"Open wider!" Ralph yells.

"Ahh caaaaaannn't!" I splutter.

"Open wider!"

"Ahh said, ahh caaaaaannn't!"

"What?"

"Ghet zout ov muh mouf!"

Ralph swims out of my mouth and

frowns at me. "Harry, I can't understand what you're saying. Why are you
speaking in code?"

Now that Ralph is out of my mouth, I
can speak normally again. "I can't open
my mouth wider!" I say. "If you went in
any farther, you'd be able to shake fins
with my rear!"

It's the first day of the school vacation and my best friends, Joe and Ralph, and I are supposed to be on our way to Shark Park. But Joe has made us stop so he can go into Kois "R" Us for the latest set of koi carp cards, and Ralph has taken the opportunity for a feed.

Ralph narrows his eyes. "How else am I supposed to get my breakfast? I'm a pilot fish, and pilot fish eat the leftover food from between sharks' teeth. It's how we've always done it, and I don't see why we should change now."

"I'm not saying we should change it. I just don't want to swallow you!"

Ralph flicks his tail angrily. "Well, if you'd saved me some of your prawn flakes in your front teeth, maybe I wouldn't have to go searching the back of your mouth for bits of last night's dinner."

I poke around at the back of my mouth with my tongue and flip out two pieces of yesterday's clamburger. Ralph gobbles them up greedily, then floats in front of me, looking hopeful.

"That's all there is," I say as Joe swims out of the store empty tentacled. "They don't get the new cards in till tomorrow," Joe says miserably.

"Well, I'm going to need something

else to stop my tummy from rumbling," Ralph moans. "Half a prawn flake and two crumbs of clamburger aren't enough for a growing pilot fish."

Ralph and Joe swim off toward Shark Park. I hope they cheer up before we get there. Vacations are supposed to be fun, but they're not if your best friends are moping around like a couple of bluefish.

As we get to the park gates Joe turns to me. "Do we have to go in?" he asks gloomily. "I still haven't recovered from what happened last time."

Ralph starts to giggle at the memory

and, I have to admit, it was pretty funny.
What happened last time was this:

1. Joe jumped on the wrecked-ship's-wheel merry-go-round,
   but he hadn't realized how fast it was going.
2. He came flying off.
3. He shot right up the slime-algae slide
   THE WRONG WAY . . .
4. He catapulted around the whale-rib swings
   SIXTEEN times, and then . . .
5. He landed with a huge TWANG on the seahorse-
   on-a-spring . . .
6. Which BOINGED him right up toward the surface
   of the sea like an out-of-control jellycopter!

If it hadn't been for Ralph and me swimming up as fast as we could to catch him, Joe would have plopped right out into the air. And everyone knows how bad being in the air is for a jelly-fish—the heat of the sun can turn them crispy in seconds.

Joe eyes the sign by the gate suspi-ciously. The sign says SHARK PARK— FAMILY FUN FOR EVERYONE!

"Hmm, I don't call being spun around like my mom's laundry fun," Joe mutters. "I don't call being thrown through the water upside down fun!"

I decide not to tell Joe that watching

129

him get flung around the park was fun
for Ralph and me.

I look around Shark Park—at the
merry-go-round, the slide, the swings,
and the seahorse—and then
I look at Joe, who is

folding each of his arms over the other. One by one. This is going to take a very long time, so I hold up a fin. "Okay, okay," I say, "we'll do something else."

To be honest, I don't know why I suggested Shark Park in the first place. It's vacation for all the kids in Shark Point, not just us three. That means the place is stuffed to the gills with fish and sharks and dolphins and octopi. So I turn back to Ralph and Joe. "It's already full," I say. "It'll be ages before we can get on the whale-rib swings, and they're the best thing in the park." Ralph and Joe nod, so I continue. "We're all too old to go on the seahorse-on-a-spring." Ralph nods. Joe hides behind Ralph, and his bottom toots. I know he's trying to be brave, but the Seahorse TWANGING incident did

132

scare him quite a bit. "The only thing left for us to do would be to go and play on the sea grass, but lots of girl fish—"

"Yuck," say Joe and Ralph together at the mention of girls.

"—are playing flounders." (Flounders is like baseball but you hit a sea urchin with a bat made from a swordfish nose.)

I don't tell Ralph and Joe my last reason for wanting to leave, because I don't want to look like a scaredy-catfish. Rick Reef and Donny Dogfish are bound to be in Shark Park today, and I really don't want to swim into them. Rick is a black-tip reef shark in our class at school, and

his favorite subject is trying to annoy me. He is very good at it. In fact, you could say he is an A student when it comes to making fun of hammerheads.

Ralph and Joe nod in agreement.

"Staying in Shark Park is going to be boring," says Ralph.

"And probably deadly," Joe adds grimly. So we turn around and head back into Shark Point.

The town is swarming with kids too— all just as bored as we are.

We fin our way down the main street. There are complaining fish being dragged into stores by their moms, and a bunch

of tough-looking scallops hanging out on the corner of Coral Drive. They're trying to be cool by blowing toots out of the sides of their shells in tune to the music coming out of Anchovy's Arcade. The three of us swim past them pretty quickly, hoping not to catch their eye.

As I watch a kid dolphin being yelled at by his grumpy-looking dad I realize that it could be a lot worse. At least I get to hang out with my friends. At least I'm not being dragged around town by my dad. Luckily, my dad is mayor of Shark Point so he hardly ever gets any time off. Which means I never have to be dragged around by him during school break. I can't imagine anything worse.

Except . . .

"Harrrrrrrrrrrrrrrrrrrrrrrrrrrrry!"

Suddenly I can.

Oh no!

It's Mom! She's swimming as fast as

she can toward us. "I thought you boys were going to Shark Park," she says as she reaches us, taking a large polka-dotted handkerchief from her finbag and wiping something off my lip.

"Booger," she whispers. But she might as well have shouted it. Ralph and Joe both heard, and they're laughing so hard behind their fins and tentacles that I think they might choke.

Mom then makes it even worse by grabbing my fin and pulling me away. "Well, since you're not in the park, you can come with me to see your dad opening the center."

My tummy sinks twenty fathoms and I try to pull away, but Mom is holding me too tight. All I can see ahead is Mom pulling me along, and all I can hear behind is Ralph and Joe giggling.

Mom and Dad always want me to come and see him opening stuff and making speeches. Usually, I can find a way out of it, but not this time. Now I wish we'd stayed in Shark Park!

We turn a corner onto Starfish Square, and I see a huge crowd of fish and squid cheering outside the gleaming new Shark Point Sports Center. There is a flag billowing from the roof and banners hung above the door. *Click! Click! Click!* Electric-eel photographers flash their electric-eel tail cameras at the doors of the sports center as my dad proudly swims to the front of the crowd.

He waves his fin and taps his nose on the waiting microphone to make sure it's working.

Mom finally lets go of me so she can clap her fins and whistle at Dad. Seriously, I don't know where to look. I can feel my cheeks start to turn red as Ralph and Joe look at me and back to Dad. Dad is a popular mayor, but he can be really embarrassing sometimes. Ralph and Joe know this, and I can see they're waiting for him to say or do something stupid so they can pull my fin about it for the rest of the week.

Mom just keeps waving at Dad and

pointing at me so that he can see I'm ı.

Dad waves back enthusiastically, and the eels all turn their cameras on me! I can feel myself turning redder than the reddest red snapper as Mom throws her fin around me and tells me to "smiley-wile." That's when Ralph and Joe fall over backward and almost die from laughing. This is the worst thing EVER!

"Yes, um, well—hello!" shouts Dad in his usual absentminded way. "Um, yes, well, I would like to welcome you all here today . . ."

Don't do it!

"But before we begin . . ."

Dad. Please. Don't do it!

"I'd just like to say that seeing you all here has reminded me . . ."

Nope. He's going to do it. He's going to tell one of his awful jokes. I try to hide under Ralph and Joe.

"Why did the deaf frog come to hear my speech today?"

Silence.

"Because"—and here Dad chuckles to himself—"because he thought I was going to be opening a Warts Center!"

No one laughs besides Mom. But Dad doesn't realize that his joke has gone down quicker than the *Titanic* and just continues as if nothing has happened. "So I duly declare the Shark Point Sports Center o—"

A piece of yellow seaweed drifts toward Dad's face and catches him in the eye. As he raises a fin to wipe it away, he accidentally slices the OPENING TODAY! ribbon that's stretched across the doors. Before he has a chance to say "—pen!" he is bounced out of the way by the rushing crowd and sent spinning up to the roof of the center, where he gets tangled in the flag and stuck to the flagpole!

I watch in horror as the photographers focus their cameras on Dad. Mom squeals and swims up to try and untangle him from the flagpole as the cameras flash and flash and flash.

I know what's going to be on the front page of the *Seaweed Times* tomorrow—my dad wrapped around the flagpole like a shark kebab. And that means every-one in Shark Point is going to be laugh-ing at him. And laughing at me

for having such an embarrassing dad!

I pull Joe and Ralph away.

I have to pull them because they've been laughing so much they've forgotten how to swim.

It's not until we're all the way on the other side of town by the movie theater that their laughing stops. And finally I see something that cheers me up.

Outside the movie theater is a huge poster of Gregor the Gnasher's first movie, *Parrot Fish of the Caribbean*, in which he plays Captain Jack Sprat, the action hero. In the poster he's wrestling with a giant squid. Gregor is my

total hero. Mom calls him 'that tooth-head', but she doesn't understand—he's the Underwater Wrestling Champion of the World and now he's started making movies. He's a total legend. It must be so cool to be a famous great white. I bet Gregor's kids don't ever get embarrassed by him.

I would have said, *Let's go and see the movie!* but I haven't gotten my

allowance yet, and with Dad currently stuck on the roof of the sports center, it wasn't about to happen anytime soon. So we keep swimming until eventually, with nowhere else to go and nothing else to do, we end up outside the library.

"The library?" says Ralph. "Talk about double boring."

"Well, what else can we do?" I say.

Thankfully, Joe comes to my rescue. "It's probably the safest place to go," he says. "Unless, of course, a bookcase falls on our heads."

I slap a fin across my face. It would

be less work to be in school! But I lead them both inside anyway.

At least there's no chance of running into Rick and Donny in the library. Rick's only interest in books is how hard he can throw them at my hammerhead when Mrs. Shelby isn't looking.

So now we're sitting in the silent library, too bored to even pick up a book.

"Is it lunchtime yet?" Ralph whispers, looking at my teeth.

"The edges of those books look quite sharp," Joe mumbles, twiddling his tentacles nervously. "I think we'd better just sit here and not move."

Great. It's the first day of vacation and we're stuck in the library doing impressions of rocks.

I sigh, and try to think of something cool to do in silence that doesn't involve moving.

When . . .

"Woooooooooooooooooooooooooooooooooooooooooooooooooooo!!!"

The shriek shatters the quiet, and I spin around in my chair, expecting to see Rick Reef waving a spider crab in front of a kid squid or something. But it's not, it's Pearl and Cora, the dolphin twins. They're dancing around and around, high-finning and shrieking, looking at their aqua-phones, looking at each other, then looking back at their aqua-phones, then looking at each other and . . .

"Wooooooooooooooooooooooooooooooooooooooooooooooooooooo!!!"-ing again.

The librarian, Mr. Gape, an elderly basking shark, heaves himself out of his chair and swims over to Pearl and Cora. "Will you two please be quiet? This is a library, not an amusement park!"

"But—" says Pearl.

"There's—" says Cora.

Mr. Gape holds up a huge fin to shush them. "Not another word, or I must ask you to leave."

"We were leaving anyway," says Pearl.

"Oh really?" says Mr. Gape.

"Yes," says Cora. "We've got some-where way more interesting to go than this boring old library!"

"And what, may I ask, could be more interesting than a library?" Mr. Gape

bellows, causing several people to drop their books in shock.

"Something," Pearl says, her voice rising toward another shriek, "that we've just seen on the interwet!"

"What?" demands Mr. Gape.

"Leggy air-breathers! They've been spotted just off Shark Point, and they're making a movie! Wooooooooooooooooooooooooooo!!!" Pearl and Cora rush past us, spinning Joe around three times and knocking Ralph and me down in their wake.

But I don't care about getting knocked over. I have too many things on my mind.

1. A movie?

2. A movie????

3. (And every OTHER number!) A MOVIE????

This vacation just got interesting!!!!

CHAPTER 2

"Let's go," I say the minute Pearl and Cora leave the building.

Joe looks at me and frowns. "I want to stay here with the nice, safe books!"

I look at Ralph.

"Who wants to see a movie being made?" he says lamely. "I don't, movies are like books that move, and we know how boring books are. I think I'd rather stay here with all the . . . books . . . " His voice trails off, not being able to think of any more mindless reasons not to leave the library. Ralph's been afraid of leggy air-breathers ever since he accidentally got caught in one of their nets.

"We'll just go and take a look, okay?" I say. "We won't go anywhere near the leggies, I promise. Cross my swim blad-der and hope to fry."

Ralph isn't convinced, but I'm desperate to follow Cora and Pearl. "I will keep you both totally and utterly and completely safe."

"Do you promise?" says Joe.

I nod my hammerhead—and nearly knock Mr. Gape over. "I promise. And afterward I'll go and get something to eat," I add, looking at Ralph.

Ralph's eyes glaze over hungrily. "Will you get sardine nuggets?"

I nod.

"With a portion of plankton?"

"Yes. With a portion of plankton."

"A super-size portion of plankton?"

"Yes!" I say impatiently. If we don't get going, we'll never catch up with Pearl and Cora.

"All right, then," says Ralph reluctantly.

"All right, then," says Joe, even more reluctantly.

But I don't care how reluctant they are—they've said yes and that's all that counts.

And now we're going to see a movie being made. A *movie*! How cool is that? My heart leaps like a bar of soap from wet fins at the thought!

I speed down the street, refusing to let go of Joe. Ralph is doing his best to keep up, but because he's such a little fish he can't kick as hard as I can, so I wrap my free fin around him and let him hitch a ride as I kick and kick and kick.

"But the leggies!" yells Joe. "What if they catch us and eat us . . . or worse?"

"They're making a movie," I say, "not trying to catch us and eat us."

"But what if they're making a movie *about* catching and eating us?" whines Joe.

He might have a point there, but I don't want him to know that. So I change the subject. "What if Gregor the Gnasher is there? What if he's the star?"

I think back to the poster for *Parrot Fish of the Caribbean* and the picture of Gregor wrestling with the giant evil squid. I wonder what it must be like to actually be in a movie. I imagine that it's me up there on the poster and that I'm a world-famous movie star who lives in a huge house in Driftywood (where all the famous movie stars work and live). I start to grin as I picture being fed peeled shrimp twenty-four hours a day by my butlers, Rick Reef and Donny Dogfish!

But then it all goes wrong.

Suddenly, on the poster, the giant squid has grabbed me by the tail and he's using my

hammerhead to bang nails into the side of a ship! My face starts to turn red, and I feel stupid for even dreaming that I could ever be cool enough to be a movie star.

Thankfully, I forget about my hammerhead once the huge, dark, open ocean approaches and we leave Shark Point behind. I can see the sunlight glinting on the tops of the waves.

The beautiful yellow light shimmers in time with the toots coming from Joe's rear as he gets more and more frightened. I look down at him, and he turns red, then blue, and then even yellower than normal.

Jellyfish do that when they're scared.

In the distance, Cora and Pearl are swimming as fast as they can. Normally, I'm one of the fastest swimmers around, but with Ralph and Joe slowing me down I'm finding it hard to keep up. Pearl and Cora are not only swimming around each other and high-finning when they come close, but they're also

double-ending and tail-swapping as they go.

Up ahead I can see the shadow of a boat bobbing and skipping on the waves. As I look closer I can see a light brighter than the sun shining in the sea. There's a leggie dangling in the water, dressed in a rubbery wet suit. She's holding a massive light and swinging it around like the lighthouse on the shore above Shark Point.

SPLOSH!!!

Another leggie crashes into the water and I can see he's holding a

162

movie camera. He's moving around, all excited, and pointing to the light-holding leggie. He wants her to shine the light over toward me!

My heart starts to pound. I let go of Ralph and Joe, smooth down my hammer with my fin, and give my best sharky grin.

The light shines right in my eyes and I strike a pose—just as heroic as Gregor in the poster, if a little hammer-ier.

But then it goes dark again as the light in my eyes moves away.

I look around, wondering what's going on. Here I am, all ready for them, but they're pointing their camera and light in completely the wrong direction!

And then I see what happened.

My heart sinks like an anchor.

There, in the spotlight, flexing his fin muscles and pointing his tail, is Rick Reef! He's triple-nosing from the slickest fin slide into the über-coolest gill slam I have ever seen. Even I have to admit it is pretty amazing, and I feel the bottom fall out of my world.

Just as the world falls out of Joe's rear.

"Sorry!" he says.

"Shh!" I hiss at him. Rick finishes on an old-school reverse dorsal, spins on his tail, and throws his fins wide.

Not only are the leggies following Rick's every move with the camera, but Cora and Pearl are screaming, "Rick! Rick! Rick!" in their best cheerleader voices.

"I guess we'd better go, then," says Ralph gloomily. "No one's gonna want to film us if we're up against Rick."

I hold up my fin. "Not so fast. I haven't

even started yet. There's no way I'm going to let Rick steal the spotlight. He's not the only shark in Shark Point!"

I kick away from Ralph and Joe until I am right under the shadow of the boat.

That's when Rick notices me.

He keeps smiling and waving to the camera with his fin, but under his breath, he says, "Swim on home, Anchor Face. They're not here to film a dork show. They want real sharks, like me."

I grit my teeth and flip into a double-endy.

"Harry," calls Joe, "be careful! That

boat has propellers. You don't want to end up getting demolished!"

Rick laughs. "See? Even your friends think you're a clumsy dork."

In the background, I can hear Donny Dogfish, Rick's sidekick, laughing behind his fin. I glare at him, trying to look tough, but it just makes my eyes cross and he laughs even more.

Cora and Pearl are still chanting, and suddenly I feel really annoyed. I'll show those dolphins, Rick, and most important, the leggies, exactly what a hammerhead can do.

I push past Rick right into the camera's

light. Curling up my tail and taking a deep breath, I begin.

This is what happens:

1. I do a perfect nose stall.
2. Rick chuckles and busts three gill slams.
3. Gritting my teeth harder, I swoosh a double inside-outy.
4. Rick shouts, "Easy!" Then he does exactly the same thing and finishes on an almost impossible outside-inny!
5. I race toward the boat's shadow and curl a wicked single flip.
6. Joe is shouting at me to calm down, but I'm not listening.

7. Rick is right behind me, doing a full-on eyes-closed belly rush!

8. Joe screams something about me getting too close to the boat.

9. I yell at Joe to be quiet and fall backward into a desperate upside-down devil smash.

10. I can see that the leggies love it. They are swinging their light this way and that, following Rick and me with the camera.

11. Rick starts whizzing in tighter and tighter circles. I can't believe what Rick is planning to do. . . . He wouldn't! He couldn't!

Rick does! I don't believe it!

He bursts out of the middle of a swirl of bubbles and heads straight toward the surface. I can see him looking back at me with big wild eyes, as he kicks with his tail as hard as he possibly can.

Cora and Pearl are cheering him on. Even Joe and Ralph are watching with their mouths hanging open as Rick whoooooooshes past the leggies and BREAKS THE SURFACE!!!!!!

Through the sparkling waves I can see his shivering shadow twisting in the air above the ocean. He does a graceful double nosey and tail touch, then SPLASHES back into the water. The leggies go crazy.

That's it!

Spin. Kick. Spin. Kick. SPIN. KICK. SPIN! KICK!! SPIN!!! KICK!!!!

BANG!!!!!!!

I'm heading for the surface too. I'm going double . . . no, three . . . no, four times faster than Rick did. I'm heading up toward the sunlight with Pearl and Cora's screams and Joe's "Noooooooooooooooooo-ooooooooooooooooooooooooo!!!" ringing in my ears.

SPLLLLLAAAAAAAAAAAAAAAAASH-HHHHHHHHHHHHHHHHH!!! I break the surface and I'm out into the air!

Flying higher and higher.

I know exactly the trick I want to bust. A triple-goofy gill slap and tail flip.

I twist and kick, still rising. Twisting. Turning. Feeling the wind on my sides, smelling the unfamiliar salty air, feeling the rush over my hammer as I ripple and twist.

I've done it! A full stunt above the waves, in mid-air with room to spare.

There's no way the cameras are still going to be on Rick.

I'm gonna be a STAR!!!!!

Well, I would have been a star if it hadn't been for the following six things. . . .

1. I'd come out of the water too fast.

2. I'd pushed up too high.

3. I hadn't thought about my re-entry after the tail flip.

4. And . . .

5. And . . .

6. Oh.

I crash down out of the sky and land with a wet, breathless slap—right on the deck of the boat!

CHAPTER 3

I don't know who's screaming louder, me or the leggies. They're running in every direction, waving their hands in the air in panic. I'm on my front, trying to flip myself off the side, back into the water, and realizing that I can't breathe!

This is bad. Really bad.

If I had time and wasn't about to suffo-
cate to death, I'd slap myself in the head
with my tail for being so brainless.

All I can see are running legs, and
all I can feel is the hot sun on my back
and it is starting to dry me out! I have
to admit to myself that Joe was right,
which makes the whole situation even
worse.

I try yelling to the leggies to help me,
but all that comes out is a terrifying hiss
that seems to scare them even more.
A couple of them even look like they're
about to throw themselves in the water
to get away from me. I think they change

their minds when they realize that there might be one shark on the boat, but there are hundreds in the ocean.

I manage to get one fin underneath me and lift my head a little, so I can see more of what's going on. I look around and see that most of the leggies are huddled at one end of the boat. There are two more leggies, a man and a woman, climbing out of the water. One of them puts down a camera and the other a huge light and they start waving their arms. They're the filmmakers from the water!

I don't think this is the best time

for me to show off, but I do try to give them a smile.

The woman screams and the man leaps back and nearly falls into the water. I close my mouth and frown. Why are they so scared? But once I have my mouth closed, they get a little braver and start coming

toward me with their hands outstretched.

Slowly, I try to move forward using my fins and tail, but I just fall back on my belly with a slap. The two leggies coming toward me take a small step back, as if they expect me to bite them. I wish I could explain to them that I'm really not interested in eating them. I JUST WANT TO GET BACK IN THE WATER!!!

I look at them with each eye on the end of my hammer and try my best to lie still. The leggies look at each other, nod, and start walking toward me again.

It's getting really difficult to breathe now, and I'm finding it hard to stay calm.

The leggies grab hold of my fins and drag me to the side of the boat.

The wood of the deck tickles my belly and I let out a giggle, which comes out sounding a little like an angry hiss. The leggies let go again, and I have to think of something really sad to stop the giggling. I picture Rick posing on a movie poster. It makes me feel angry rather than sad, but at least it keeps me from laughing.

The leggies grab me again and take me right to the edge of the boat. I swivel my eyes around and see that the really scared leggies are getting a little braver now. They edge closer to get a better look. The leggies heave me onto the side of the boat. I can see the ocean, all wet and inviting below me, and then the other leggies coming toward me.

A few of them are brave enough to give me a little stroke before I get pushed back into the water.

Thank Cod! I can breathe again!

181

But as the bubbles clear, all I can hear is laughter.

Rick is right in my face, clutching his sides with his fins. Big, fat laughs are coming out of his mouth in huge snorts. Behind him, Cora and Pearl are laughing too. They have their fins across each other's shoulders, and they are

laughing so much I think they're going to be sick.

"There he goes!" calls Rick as I swim away as fast as I can. "The shark so clumsy he can't miss a tiny boat in the middle of the ocean! You'd better get those hammerhead sensors looked at, Harry. They're obviously as cruddy as the rest of you!"

Red-faced and with hot tears in my eyes, I swim and swim and swim. I can hear Ralph and Joe calling me, but I don't care. I have to get out of here.

"How useless are hammerhead sharks?" Rick shouts after me. "A whole bunch of leggies to chew on, and he lets them push him back into the sea. Me, I'd love to eat a leggy air-breather if I got the chance. Not Harry, though. Harry is their *pet!*"

I don't stop for anyone until I get home.

I can hear Mom in the kitchen. Dad probably won't be back from his office yet—or he's still trapped on the sports center roof—so I might be able to sneak in without anyone noticing.

But as I try to skulk past the kitchen, my catfish swims over and starts purring loudly.

"Is that you, angelfish?" Mom calls from the kitchen.

I hate it when she calls me that.

"No," I say. "It's the Most Dorky Shark in the History of the Sea, and the leggy air-breathers have it all on film to prove it!"

Mom comes out of the kitchen, wiping her fins on a dish towel. "What are you talking about?"

So I tell her.

When I finish, Mom wraps her fins around me and cuddles me close.

I hate it when she does that, too.

Why can't she just leave me alone?

Can't she see I want to go to my room and sulk?

Mom wets the edge of her sea sponge with her tongue and wipes some seaweed from my face.

"Sounds like you've had a rotten day. Why don't I make you a lovely dinner and then you can soak in the hot spring and I'll scrub your back, like I did when you were a baby? I have a really lovely new sea-urchin scrubber. You used to love that."

Could my day get any worse?

Well, yes, it could.

Mom makes me sit in the kitchen while she cooks dinner. "Since you're so upset,

186

I've made you a whole plate of leggie-shaped fish cakes and coral crunchies! They'll make you all better."

My dinner is so babyish that not even Ralph would be willing to clean it from between my teeth.

Not that I care about Ralph anymore. Or Joe.

I don't want to see anyone ever again. I'm way too ashamed.

When Mom isn't looking, I pour the leftovers out the window and make it look like I've cleared my plate. Mom goes straight back to the stove. "That's my hungry little starfish! I'll make you some more."

I hold up a fin. "No thanks, Mom," I say. "That was great, but I'm full and I'm tired. I think I just need to go to bed."

"What a sensible little starfish!" Mom beams. "How about I sing you a lullaby, then? That always cheers you up." I open my mouth but it's too late. *"Rock-a-bye Harry, on the sea top,"* she shrieks.

Aaaaaaaaaah! Of all the lullabies in existence, why did she have to pick the one that mentions the sea top?

"I've got to go, Mom," I say, swimming for the door. Mom blocks my way with her hammerhead and gives me a big, slobbery kiss. I close my eyes and wish that I was in a terrible nightmare. At least then I'd be able to wake up. But I'm not in a nightmare. Mom pats me on the hammerhead and finally lets me go. I swim to my bedroom so fast my dopey head gets jammed in the door-way. Once I finally make it in, I slam the door and throw myself on the bed.

What a rotten, ROTTEN day!

I don't think I've ever been so embarrassed. Not even when Dad accidentally tripped on Queen Aquae the Third's robe and fell into her lap on LIVE TELEVISION!

That's it, I think, *I'm not going out again for this whole entire vacation.* If I don't go out again, I won't see my dad making a fool of himself as he tries to open stuff and make stupid speeches, and I won't bump into Rick and the dolphin twins. And I won't be filmed making a complete fool of myself.

There's tons I could be doing at home anyway. It won't be that bad to stay indoors for the vacation, will it? I mean, I'm a clever shark—I can find lots to do. I'll make a list to show you.

1. Um, I could . . .

2. No wait, I know . . .

3. It might be a good idea if . . . no . . . um.

4. This is turning out to be a much harder list to make than I imagined.

Whatever.

I don't care if I'm so thick headed that

I can't even make a list of what to do while I'm all thick headed!

> 5. I'm staying in my room for the whole
>
> vacation and that's that!

CHAPTER 4

Hmmmmmmmmmmm!

I don't want to open my eyes.

Hmmmmmmmmmm!! Hmmmmmm!!

I'm not going to open my eyes. I snuggle deeper into my bed and flip more seaweed blankets over me with my tail.

Hmmmmmmmmmm!! Hmmmmm!! Hmmmm!!!

Then a bright light starts flickering in front of my eyelids, making the darkness all pink.

The light just reminds me of the film crew in the sea yesterday. I put the pillow over my head.

"Come *hmmmmmm* on, Harry. *Hmmmmm* it's time to *hmmmmmmmm* get up!" Humphrey, my humming-fish

alarm clock, is humming right in my ear. I'd been in such a bad mood last night I'd forgotten to ask him not to wake me up at the usual time.

"Leave me alone," I say from beneath the blankets.

"But it's time to rise and SHINE!" says Lenny, my lantern fish, shining his light right at my closed eyes again. He's swum under the blankets to point his light at me. Lenny and Humphrey are really useful when it comes to getting up in the morning, when you want to get up. But when you don't want to get up ever again, they're a real pain.

"Look!" I shout, pushing back the blankets and roaring up out of the bed. "I'm not getting up!"

Humphrey *hmmmmms* quietly and Lenny flickers softly. Humphrey raises his fin. "I . . . I don't want to argue with you, but you've, um . . . just gotten up."

He's right. I am out of bed.

Which is *exactly* what I didn't want to do.

Why does everything keep going wrong?

On top of that, I can hear someone coming down the hall outside my bedroom. It'll be Mom, with a special breakfast to cheer me up.

I. Want. To. Scream.

As the door opens, I dart back into bed and signal to Humphrey and Lenny to be quiet with a dark look that makes them both shiver.

It is Mom, but she doesn't have breakfast.

"Morning, angelfish."

Humphrey and Lenny start snickering behind their fins.

"I just wanted to tell you," Mom goes on, smoothing down the corners of my blanket, "that Ralph and Joe have been asking for you."

The last two people I want to see.

I groan.

Mom stops smoothing. "What's up, angel?"

I think quickly . . . then flop my fins out wide and stick out my tongue. Mom peers at it. I can see Humphrey and Lenny shaking their heads and hiding their faces in their fins. "I don't feel well," I say, flipping my tail slowly and painfully and coughing a little.

Humphrey can't help himself and *hmmmms* in disgust, but I flick him a "pipe down" look from the other end of my hammer as Mom places a fin on my forehead to take my temperature.

"I don't think I can even swim to the kitchen for breakfast," I say, coughing again.

"Well, you don't have a temperature," Mom says. "But if you don't feel well, you'd better stay home, and I'll put the sea-cow steaks I had out for breakfast back in the fridge."

Sea-cow steaks?

My tummy rumbles at the thought. But I can't get out of it now. I groan and turn over in bed as Mom leaves, saying "Maybe Dad might want them in a sandwich to take to County Hall."

Today is shaping up to be as rotten

as yesterday, and I haven't even left my room yet.

"Hey, Harry!" I hear Ralph from outside my bedroom window. "You getting up or what?"

Joe puts his tentacles through the gap in the window and unlocks the latch. The window opens wide and Ralph and Joe float in. Humphrey and Lenny float out, shaking their heads at me.

Joe hovers over the bed, counting something on his tentacles. "One, two, three, four, five, six," he counts out loud. "You do know that staying in bed all day is the seventh most dangerous thing to do in the world? What if there's a reefquake? You'll be tangled in your blankets and won't be able to get out. It's very, very dangerous staying in bed."

I push back the covers and sit up angrily. "I don't want to see anyone today. Not today, or for the rest of the vacation!"

Ralph and Joe look at each other.

"You're not still upset about yester-day, are you?" Ralph asks.

"Yes, Ralph, I am," I say, crossing my fins.

"Don't be silly," Ralph says with a smile. "Remember how we laughed at Joe when he got TWANGED off the seahorse in Shark Park? He didn't become all moody and say he didn't want to see anyone, did he?"

Well, no. He didn't.

"And," Ralph goes on, "what about when I went into the girls' bathroom by mistake on the first day of school? You and Joe laughed so hard I thought you were going to explode. But I didn't get all dopey and not talk to you, did I?"

No. He didn't.

I uncross my fins. A bit.

"Come on, Harry, it's only the second day of vacation. We have a whole week to have fun. Let's forget about yesterday."

Ralph has a point. I completely uncross my fins and get out of bed.

"All right," I say. "But we aren't going anywhere near any cameras, okay?"

Within a couple of seconds we're out the window and I'm calling to my mom in the kitchen as I swim past. "I'm going to the park with Ralph and Joe."

"But what about your cough?" Mom cries after me.

"It's much better, thanks."

"But what about your breakfast?"

"I don't want any."

"You haven't had any breakfast?" Ralph looks at me, panic-stricken.

"Nope. Sorry," I say.

"If this keeps up, I'm going to waste away! I'll shrink from a pilot fish into a pilchard, and then where will you be?"

"I don't know."

"At the dentist with rotten teeth, that's where, because I didn't clean them for you."

"All right, all right," I say. "I'll have double helpings tomorrow, okay?"

Ralph thinks about this. "Okay, but I prefer seaweedies, not prawn flakes."

I sigh and nod. "Can we get going now, please?"

All this talk about food is making my tummy moan and rumble. I wish I hadn't pretended to be sick. I wish I'd gotten my teeth around Mom's sea-cow steaks!

When we get to the park, we're the first on the swings. We even manage to get Joe to take a turn.

Joe swings up high as Ralph pushes him and I swim in front, high-finning Joe's tentacles as he comes close. But

then Ralph gives one huge push and
Joe is sent spinning right over the top
of the swing and flying straight toward
me!

PLAP. PLAP. PLAP. PLAP. PLAP. PLAP.
PLAP. PLAP. PLAP PLAP. PLAP. PLAP.
PLAP. PLAP. PLAP PLAP. PLAP. PLAP.
PLAP. PLAP. PLAP.

. . . is the sound of Joe's tentacles

sticking to my hammerhead as Joe holds on for dear life and we fall back onto the seabed.

After that, the three of us are laughing so hard that I've completely forgotten about yesterday.

Except . . .

FLUBBERRRRRRRRRRRRRRRRRRR!!!

Suddenly, my stupid hammerhead is boinging all over the place and I can't see a thing as my eyes swivel and shake.

"Hello, Rubberhead!"

It's Rick.

He's sneaked up behind me and flubbered my head with his fin. Ralph and Joe catch hold of each end of my hammer to stop the shaking.

Donny, Cora, and Pearl are there too, laughing at me as Rick circles around us. "Hey, it's Harry Hammer—the star of the funniest film of all time. Can't wait until that one HITS the theater!" laughs Rick. "It's going to be a MASSIVE SMASH, just like it was on that boat!"

Rick and Donny can hardly swim upright, they're laughing so much.

I'm about to tell Ralph and Joe that we should go and leave those two jokers behind, when suddenly something catches my nose. Sharks have the best sense of smell in the ocean, and hammerheads have some of the best senses of all the sharks, so I'm the first one to smell it.

It's a warm, fishy, tasty, yummy smell, and it's getting right in my nostrils. I can

feel it sliding right down my throat and into my very empty tummy.

It is such a delicious smell. It doesn't just make my tummy rumble, it makes it almost shake with hunger, almost as if Rick has flubbered it!

I turn away from Rick, toward the direction of the smell.

Rick is a little annoyed by this. It's not the reaction he's expecting. He fins me on the shoulder. "Hey, don't turn away when I'm laughing at you!"

But I can't concentrate. The smell and the taste are beautiful, and my tummy is telling me to follow it, whatever Rick might be saying. I kick away and use my shark sense to lock on to the delicious aroma. I can dimly hear that Rick is following me, telling anyone who'll listen what a weirdo I am.

"Harry! Wait!" calls Ralph, but I can't help myself. When a shark gets hold of a scent, especially one as tasty as this, there's no stopping them. I must find out what it is, and I don't care what else is happening!

I kick faster.

"Listen, Rubberhead, if you . . . oh . . . oh . . . WHAT IS THAT SMELL?" Rick has obviously caught the scent too.

I kick even faster. Whatever it is, I want to get to it first.

"H-H-H-Harry!!" calls Joe. "Don't go that way! It's toward the open o-o-o-ocean!"

But I'm not listening to Joe, either. All I can hear is the rumbling in my tummy, and all I can smell is the tasty scent.

"Come on, Joe, we'd better follow them!" I hear Ralph calling to Joe, but I'm too far gone. I'm out of the park now, swimming faster and faster. I can hear Rick talking as he kicks faster too. "That is the most delicious thing I've ever smelled," he says dreamily.

I kick harder. Rick is not getting there first.

Faster.

Faster.

I can feel the drool coming out of the corners of my mouth. I want that food, I want it now, and I'm going to get it FIRST!

Faster!

FASTER!!

We're right off Shark Point now, out over the seaweed fields where the shepherd fish tend their flocks. The scent is dragging us down into the forest of seaweed growing there. But it doesn't slow me down. I keep kicking and I can feel Rick's breath on my tail.

He's closing.

FASTER!!!!

FASTER!!!!

In the dim distance, I can hear Ralph and Joe shouting, "Watch out!!! Harry, WATCH OUT!!!"

And then I can hear Donny shouting too. "RICK, STOP! STOP!!!"

But the scent. It's too strong. I can't stop.

So as I burst between the thick fronds of seaweed, it's much too late to see that I'm heading straight toward two wet-suited leggies, holding lights and cameras while floating inside a huge cage!

Rick and I are going too fast to stop! We're going to crash right into them!

CHAPTER 5

What happened next is a bit confusing, as you can see from the list that follows.

2. *WHAM! CRASH!*

TWAAAAAAANNNNNGGGGG!!!

4. I go bouncing and boinging off into the deep.

3. My hammerhead doesn't get stuck. For once.

1. We both put the breaks on, but we hit the cage at FULL SPEED!

See what I mean? Completely confusing.

I've bounced off the cage and am somersaulting through the water. I flap my fins, desperately trying to slow myself down. Eventually I get control over my body, but my head is a whole other problem! It's vibrating worse than when Rick flubbers it with his fin. I shake my head and try to stop the movement, and after a few seconds the ocean stops rocking and I can start to make sense of what's happened.

The film crew has dropped a shark cage into the water and is filming from it. A shark cage isn't for catching sharks, it's to keep the leggies from getting eaten by the sharks they're filming.

"Mmmmmmmmmmmmmmmmmmm!" For a moment, I think that Humphrey has followed me all the way from home, but then I realize it's me making that noise. I look down at my tummy and I remember how hungry I am. The smell of food that drew Rick and me here at full speed is

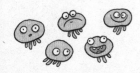

almost too strong
to bear. I turn on
my hammer-vision
and see that on the
seabed all around
the shark cage, the

leggies have poured buckets and buckets
of juicy, yummy, lovely shrimp!

They've obviously done it to get
sharks to appear, so Rick and I have
done exactly what they want. I don't
care, though. Opening my mouth wide,
I start to swim about like crazy, shovel-
ing in as much shrimp as I possibly
can.

It's the most amazing shrimp I've ever tasted, and I honestly can't get enough. The delicious scent of it is in my nostrils, and the taste going all the way down from my mouth to my rapidly filling tummy is just mind-blowing.

In fact, I'm so busy concentrating on getting as much shrimp as possible that I almost don't realize that someone is calling for help.

Swallowing hard, I turn my hammer-vision back to normal and see that Rick is caught in the bars of the cage!

The leggies seem delighted and are tickling him under the chin and patting

him on the head
as he struggles to
get free.

"Help! Help!" he
sobs. "Please get
me out of here!"

I can't help
laughing a little to
myself as I shark

down another mouthful of shrimp. Poor
Rick. I suppose I should help him, but
then I notice that the film crew is
pointing their lights and cameras right
at me.

I feel my cheeks turning red in

embarrassment as I remember what happened yesterday, and I start to cringe. I bet they're filming me because they're still making their movie about comedy sharks, and I'm clearly the most hilarious shark in the water.

I'm about to swim away and go hide, when I see the woman leggie reach down into the cage and take the lid off another fresh bucket of shrimp. She pours it into the water right in front of me, and then gives me a massive thumbs-up. She wants me to eat!

I dart forward into the cloud of tasty shrimp and barrel roll into a half fin curl.

The leggies applaud and lift their cameras and turn the lights on again. They want me to bust some more moves!

I don't need any more encouragement, and as I leap forward I have completely forgotten about yesterday and all the embarrassment. This is awesome! I'm finally getting the chance to show everyone what I can really do. I power up over the cage, twisting into a radical ninety-degree hammer shift (the move only hammerheads can do, and the one I never do around Rick because it always makes him flubber me). The leggies throw out even more shrimp as I turn that trick into a belly crunch and slide-swish right along the top of the cage.

"Harry! Harry! What about me?" calls Rick, still trying to get his head out from between the bars.

I rub past Rick and tail-tickle him, which drives the leggies crazy. They love it!

"Help! Help!" Rick cries.

"Har-ry! Har-ry!"

What?

I turn around, and I can't believe what I see. Not only have Ralph and Joe and Donny arrived, but Cora and

Pearl have followed them out of the park, and the dolphin twins are chant-ing *my* name!

Ralph and Joe are clapping along as Cora and Pearl chant.

"Har-ry! Har-ry!!"

And I'm off again, swishing up past the cage. Using my hammer as an extra fin, so that I can turn quicker and tighter than any other shark, I twist into an ever-tighter spiral.

Building up speed.

Faster

Faster.

Just like yesterday. But this time I'm going to be heading down.

Faster!

FASTER!!!!

And then *BANG!*

With the sun above me lighting the water in an explosion of glittering

sparkles, I race down toward the cameras and the cage. I triple-gill, run three simultaneous back pikes, and roll into a totally cool three-quarter gnash master. With a whoop and a yell I fall past the cage, do a complete body stall, a gnarly nose-endy, a floaty inside-outy that goes straight into a perfect outside-inny that Rick would have been over the moon to pull, and then, to finish off, using the edge of my hammer as a lever, I POP Rick right out of the bars and out into the open water!

The leggies are going crazy. The light is on me, they're following my every

move with the camera, and they're kicking their last buckets of shrimp into the
water all around me.

I spin up, openmouthed, through the
shrimp, eating every bit.

As I turn back to the cage, I fold
my fin across my now-full tummy
and bow to the cage and the leggies
inside. They've dropped their cameras
and lights and are just applauding and
cheering along with Ralph, Joe, Cora,
and Pearl.

Rick doesn't hang around. I can see
from his cheeks that he is just as
embarrassed as I was yesterday. He

pulls Donny away from the group and heads back toward Shark Point.

"Hey, Rick," Pearl calls out as he slinks away, "bet you wish you were a hammerhead, don't you? That way your pointy head wouldn't have gotten stuck in the cage."

Cora giggles. "I can see how much you scared those leggies, too. They were so scared, they could only tickle you under the chin!"

Soon Rick and Donny can no longer be seen.

And everyone else is laughing and cheering with me.

Except Ralph.

Ralph has pried open my mouth and is eyeing all the bits of shrimp stuck between my teeth.

"Breakfast at last!" he yells as he dives in!

CHAPTER 6

Ralph, Joe, and I are just about the last Shark Pointers to get into the movie theater tonight. It is absolutely packed.

We thread our way carefully between the rows, trying to get to our seats before the movie starts. I ache all over from those moves I pulled for the leggies in

the shark cage earlier. It'll be a while before I do anything like that again, but it was a whole lot of fun.

I have a humongous tub of shrimpopcorn, and Ralph's got two, having decided to take a night off from eating stuff from between my teeth. I think this has more to do with the fact that Dad has finally given me my allowance and I am paying!

Joe is too scared of the shrimpopcorn machine to get close enough to pick up a tub, so he had some "nice, safe ice cream instead, not too cold, though, because I don't want to get a frostbitten tentacle."

As we get to our seats I see that Cora and Pearl are two rows in front of us. They've got their aqua-phones on and are seaberry messaging all their friends. Cora catches sight of me and fins Pearl, who looks up. They both smile and wave. Then they hold up their aqua-phones and I see that they're not just messaging their friends, they're posting pictures and videos of me pulling all those stunts on to Plaicebook!

I, of course, turn red. But luckily, in the dim light of the theater, no one knows except me.

Phew!

Girls.

I sit down between Joe and Ralph, just as the lights go down and the movie begins.

WHAM!!!

Gregor is there on the screen, all huge and white and toothy. And pretty soon he's wrestling squids, and sword-fighting narwhals and racing to save the damsel-fish in distress.

It's great watching Gregor up on the screen, and for a moment I think about my two days in front of the camera being a movie star. Yeah, it was great for a while, but when I think about my . . .

1. Aching fins (ouch)
2. Bruised hammer (ouchy)
3. All the flubbering Rick did with my hammerhead (ouchy boingy)
4. Pictures of me appearing EVERYWHERE (cringey)
5. How tired I feel right now (zzzzz)

   . . . all because of one small movie I was accidentally in, I think that maybe I just don't have the energy to do it full-time zzzzzzzzzz . . .

Ralph and Joe wake me up at the end of *Parrot Fish of the Caribbean.*

As we swim back home I realize that even though I don't want to be a world-famous movie star anymore, and even though I missed my hero Gregor's first-ever movie, at least one fintastic thing has happened. This vacation hasn't been boring at all!

Squid-napped!

CHAPTER 1

Vroooooooooooooooooooooooooooooooo ooooooooooooooom!

Vrooooooooooooooooooooooooooo ooooooooooooooooooooooooooom!

Vrooooooooooooooooooooooooooo oooooooooooooooooooooooooooom!

I'm floating at the side of Turbo Terry's

Turtle-kart Track as the turtle-karts whiz
past. It's making my hammerhead eyes
go double goggly.

"Don't look at me like that!' says Rick Reef, who is float- ing next to me. The pointy-faced reef shark (who is my number one enemy) waits until everyone is look- ing the other way,

then pings the side of my head with the edge of his fin.

"Hey-y-y-y-y-y! I can't help looking at you like that," I say, trying to stop my hammer from flubbering. "I have eyes on each side of my head! I look at everything—whether I want to or not. And in your case it's definitely *not*."

Rick pulls up the collar on his leather jacket. He always does this when he wants to look tough. "Yeah, but you don't have to be so starey about it."

"It's the turtle-karts. They're going so fast, they're making my eyes all weird."

Vroooooooooooooooooooooooooooooo oooooooooooooooooooooooooooooom!

Vroooooooooooooooooooooooooooo oooooooooooooooooooooooooooooom!

Vroooooooooooooooooooooooooooo oooooooooooooooooooooooooooooom!

Three more turtle-karts zoom around the bend, their flippers whizzing like speedboat propellers and the electric eels underneath zapping up extra power for speed. Riders are hanging on to the turtle's backs with their fins or tentacles, all wearing brightly colored crash helmets with cool dragonfish or super squid cartoons on the side. I have to admit that this trip to Turbo Terry's Turtle-kart Track could have been really fantastic, if it hadn't been for five rotten things. . . .

1. It's my birthday. I hate my birthday. (No, really, I do. You'll see why later.)

2. Mom and Dad have taken us all to the turtle-kart track. (You think that's good? Think again, because . . .)

3. Mom and Dad are staying to watch! (How uncool is that? So uncool you can make hot sea-cucumber kebabs out of it.)

4. Everyone is noticing Dad because he's the mayor of Shark Point and he's telling everyone it's his number one son's birthday! (Daaaaaaaaaaaaaaad! Don't!)

5. And worst of all, Dad thought it was a good idea to invite my whole class—including Rick Reef (number one enemy) and Donny Dogfish (number one enemy's sidekick and general pain in the tail).

I did try to persuade Dad that Rick and Donny shouldn't come turtle-karting—in fact I've done nothing but try to persuade Dad ever since the invitations went out. Even this morning, when we were getting ready to leave, I tried again. But Dad was having none of it. "As mayor of Shark Point, I want everyone to get along," he said. "I know you and Rick don't see eye to eye, but maybe bringing him along today will be the start of a beautiful friendship."

Why do grown-ups say such weird things? There's nothing beautiful or friendly about someone who wants to flubber your head all the time.

FLUBBERRRRRRRR!!!!!!

See? He's done it again!

This time Rick pings my head so hard, my best friends Ralph and Joe have to grab hold of each side of the hammer to stop it from flubbering. Rick and Donny swim off toward the turtle-kart pits, snorting with laughter. It's nearly time for our session on the track to begin, but I'm really not in the mood now. I sigh loudly—so loud it makes a passing school of sardines dive for cover.

Why did I have to be born a hammerhead? Why couldn't I have been born a great white like my all-time hero Gregor the Gnasher? No one would make Gregor the Gnasher's head TWANG like a ruler on the side of a school desk—not without getting their bottom bitten off, anyway.

Gregor is the bravest, strongest shark who has ever lived. Not only is he

Underwater Wrestling Champion *of the world*, but he's also a movie star and the number-one-most-photographed-shark-under-the-sea. Three years in a row.

Ralph puts his fin on my shoulder. "Don't worry about it, Harry, just wait till we're in the karts. Rick'll be smiling on the other side of his face by the time we've beaten him on the track!"

I look at Ralph. Since he's only a pilot fish, it's hard to imagine him beating anyone on the track. He's too small to reach the controls, for a start, so we're going to have to share a kart.

I feel something quivering behind me and rotate my eyes to see my friend Joe. Joe is a jellyfish, and although he's not exactly a coward, he tries to avoid anything that might put him in danger. And since he's very good at finding out about stuff that might put him in danger, he ends up avoiding lots of things.

POP!

That's Joe thinking about karts. But

it's not his mouth that's popping, it's his backside. He does that when he's scared.

Ralph fins me in the ribs. "For Joe, karts equal farts."

Joe says, "You might laugh—"

(Which we do.)

"—but turtle-karting is the seventeenth most dangerous thing you can do on a Thursday."

"It's Saturday," Ralph points out.

"Whatever." Joe waves his tentacles around angrily, and turns a bit purple.

"Okay," I say. "Have we done the other sixteen more dangerous things today?"

Joe scratches his head with three of his thirty-six tentacles. "No."

"Then we'll be okay," I say.

"Come on, Harry!"

I turn and see Dad waving to me as he finishes signing autographs for a group of mirror carp.

"Time to get you on the track!"

I swim as slowly as I can toward the rickety old equipment shed next to the kart pits. I swim slowly because I know that soon everyone else will get really excited as they find the right racing jacket and fin gloves, but I'll just feel really embarrassed. The reason I'll

feel really embarrassed is because once everyone is in their gear, the pit chief, an old hermit crab called Nobbly, will start handing out the crash helmets.

I can feel my heart sinking like an anchor at the thought, and the water around my face warms up as my cheeks start to turn red.

Rick and Donny get cool helmets with dragonfish pictures. Ralph gets a super-cool helmet with a pirate ship on either side and a skull and crossbones on the back. Even Joe's bottom stops tooting as Nobbly hands him a helmet shaped like a swordfish's head.

"Wow!" Joe says as his tentacles fight an imaginary duel with the swordfish. Then it's my turn.

"Oh," says Nobbly. "Hmmm. A hammerhead. . . ."

Nobbly starts searching the shelves for a helmet that will fit. I can hardly bear to look. I know exactly what's going to happen.

Rick and Donny are snickering in the corner—high-finning and using their fins to make hammer shapes on the sides of their helmets.

My cheeks are now so red you could use my face to warn ships about the rocks around Shark Point.

Nobbly looks at Mom and Dad. They just smile. Dad pats me on the head with a fatherly fin. "I'm sure they've got something in your size, son."

A few minutes later I'm not just embarrassed, I'm wishing the seabed would open up and swallow me whole.

"It's okay, I'll go with Joe—there'll be more room," says Ralph, trying really hard not to laugh. Behind me, I can hear Rick and Donny snickering again.

I watch as Ralph and Joe climb into their turtle-kart.

"It's not that bad, son." Dad says.

I just bite my lip and look straight ahead.

Nobbly couldn't find a single helmet to fit over my hammer head. So instead he found *two*! As I slide into the seat and Nobbly straps me in, I catch sight of myself reflected in the window of Turbo Terry's store.

I've got a helmet over *each end* of my hammer head. They're held in place by thick lengths of seaweed tape. But the seaweed tape doesn't cover the fact that both helmets are for babies and have pink cartoon starfish on them.

Bop-de-bop-de-bop-bop-bop! Shish! Shish! Shish!

That's Rick playing bongos on the two helmets while Donny dances around me, making cymbal noises out of the corner of his mouth.

"Enough of that, you two," says Nobbly, squeezing my fin protectively with his claw. Rick and Donny swim off to their turtle-karts. Trails of gigglebubbles stream from their mouths.

"Ready?" Nobbly asks, tickling the electric eel beneath my kart to get the turtle warmed up.

"Yes, I suppose so," I say through gritted teeth.

"Gentlefish!" shouts Nobbly. "*Start your engines!*"

And we're off!

Luckily, it isn't long before I forget about the double embarrassment of the double starfish helmets and actually start to enjoy myself.

The kart track is a figure eight with an over-under section in the middle. If I steer my turtle well, I can take it at full

258

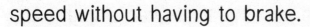

speed without having to brake.

Joe seems to be doing the best out of everyone. Because he has so many tentacles he can do about thirty-six things at once, so steering and braking at the same time is a breeze.

"Wheeeeeeeeeeeeeeeeeeeeeeeeeeeeeeeeeeeeeeee!" Joe yells with excitement as he races past the finish line, starting his second lap. Ralph is hanging on for dear life, but seems to be enjoying it too.

I overtake Donny easily and see Rick up ahead of me, just going around a bend. He's pushing the electric eel far too hard and the turtle-kart's gears are grinding in protest. The turtle itself is frowning up at Rick.

I tickle the eel in my kart and coax a little more speed out of the turtle. I'm starting to gain on Rick. I may be a hammerhead with two helmets and goggly eyes, but I'm not going to give up without a fight. I put my head down to reduce resistance against the water and flick my tail to give me a tiny bit of extra thrust. *You'd better watch out, Rick,* I say to myself. *You might be the fastest shark on the swimming team, but I'm going to prove I'm better than you at karting!*

Rick looks back over his shoulder and locks his eyes on me. I look straight back at him—as best as I can. Rick's face is all screwed up with determination, like there's no way he's going to let a hammerhead with two baby crash helmets strapped to his head get past. Yeah, well, having to wear two helmets is making me twice as determined to beat him.

I push on, continuing to catch up with Rick. When I'm almost on his tail, I see him look past me. I glance back and see that he's looking at Donny. Rick makes a signal to Donny with his tail. Donny suddenly turns his turtle and swerves around, going up the shoulder onto the upper section of the track—just as Joe and Ralph are coming past! Joe swerves and skids to a halt just before the crash barrier. Donny continues over the hump, across the other side, just as I round the corner about to overtake Rick.

Then I realize what is happening. Donny's steered himself onto a collision course with my turtle! There's nothing I can do. Donny spears into the side of me, sending me right off the track.

"You boys! Stop that at once!" Nobbly calls from the pits.

I turn the steering wheel with all my strength, but it's not enough. The turtle shell hits the crash barrier hard and we bounce back, straight into Donny. This pushes Donny into Rick and sends all three of us off the track.

KERRRRRRRRRRRR-ASH!!!!!!!!!!

The three turtle-karts spin to a halt and we lie there panting, trying to get our breath back, as Nobbly, Dad, and Mom dash over.

"Oh, my little starfish!" Mom wails.

"Are you okay, son?" Dad calls.

Nobbly tuts and mutters under his breath as he frees us from the turtle-karts, which immediately swim off in disgust. He chases after them to make sure they're okay.

"Have you hurt your hammer? Can

you swim in a straight line?" Mom cries.

"I'm fine, Mom! Don't have a sea cow." I wriggle as Mom hugs me and showers my two crash helmets with kisses.

"I think that's enough turtle-karting for today," says Dad, lifting me up off the seabed. "Time for your birthday party, I think."

I remove the helmets from each end of my hammer head and sigh. At least one thing's for sure—my party can't possibly go as badly as the turtle-karting. . . .

I have to sit at the head of the table in the restaurant. Dad is next to me, showing all his teeth in his best grin. This is because he's noticed the other diners nudging each other with their fins and whispering to each other that they're in the same restaurant as the mayor of Shark Point. Joe and Ralph are on my other side. Joe is gazing at the party food on the table in front of us. I know that the food is usually the best thing about a party, but not this party. In my head I start making a list of reasons why I don't want to eat it.

1. **Reef rolls**–there is NO way I'm eating anything that includes Rick's last name.

2. **Jelly-and-iceberg cream**– I'm not sure I can eat anything that reminds me of Joe, either.

3. **Rainbow-fish trifle**–the pink layer is exactly the same color as the awful baby helmets I had to wear.

4. **Sea-cow-cheese and sea-cucumber sandwiches**– cut by my mom into the shape of my hammer head. 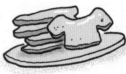 Great.

Ralph looks at my mouth. "Okay," he says. "Make sure you have some rolls, sandwiches, and trifle. I'm not excited about the jelly. It's really difficult for me to get it out from between your teeth, and even if I can get it out, it always dissolves before I can swallow it!" Ralph is a pilot fish, so he gets his food from the leftovers between my teeth.

Yes, it is as gross as it sounds.

"I thought it was *my* party food," I say to him out of the corner of my mouth.

"It might be your party food," Ralph hisses out of the corner of *his* mouth, "but it's *my* lunch."

I sigh and look down the table. Rick and Donny are at the other end. They're on their best behavior for once because of the scolding they got from Nobbly for causing the accident.

Mom is nowhere to be seen.

This makes my heart sink so low it feels like it's about to drop out of my tail. I know what's coming next and it's not going to be good.

I close my eyes and wish that I was a lone shark, like Gregor the Gnasher (when he's not busy being famous). If I was a lone shark, I wouldn't have to bother with birthday parties, because lone sharks never do anything in groups. And they definitely never have to invite their number one enemies to their birth-day parties. *Maybe it won't be that bad this year*, I say to myself. But then . . .

1.   The lights dim.
2.   Music starts to play and the angelfish waiters form a choir around me and start singing "Happy Birthday" (except they sing "*Harry* Birthday"!).
3.   Everyone in the restaurant stops eating and starts staring at me.
4.   Mom appears, carrying an enormous birthday cake.

Mom. MOM! WHAT HAVE YOU DONE!?!?

Not only is the cake huge and fluffy and layered with sparkly rows of fish eggs, but Mom has also used the pinkest of pink-plankton icing to pipe two kissing sea horses on the top, and the whole thing is lit by a candlefish.

At the other end of the table, Rick and Donny start grinning so wide, a whale could swim down their throats.

Mom places the cake right in front of me. "There you are, gorgeous. Now blow your candlefish out and make a wish!"

With my cheeks glowing as pink as the cake, I lean forward to blow out the candlefish. The candlefish looks down at me and glares.

"You're a boy," he whispers.

I nod.

The candlefish shakes his head in disgust. "I've been stuck in all this horrible icing for a boy!"

I blow a stream of air bubbles into his face, but he stays upright.

"And why have you got two sea horses kissing on your cake?"

"I don't know," I hiss, blowing another stream of bubbles into his face.

But he keeps on complaining, standing upright in the icing. "You should've had two piranhas fighting."

"Be quiet!" I yell.

And then something truly terrible happens. I lean forward to push him over,

274

but I lose my balance and topple forward, hammer head first, into the cake.

"Oh no!" Mom cries.

As I pull my head out of the cake,
great clumps of plankton icing slide
down my face.

"Harry's pink!" Rick yells.

"Like a girl," Donny says with a snicker.

"I'm out of here," the candlefish
mutters as he swims for the door.

"Quick, make your wish," Mom says,
dabbing at my head with a seaweed
napkin.

I can't stand it anymore. This has been
the worst birthday ever! Rick and Donny,

the dopey pink crash helmets, the dopey race, the dopey kart, and now the *dopey cake all over my face!*

"I wish"—I shout, getting up from the table—"I wish that it wasn't my birthday!"

Another piece of icing slides down my face and sticks to my top lip. Great. I'm wearing lipstick.

Rick and Donny can hardly float, they're laughing so hard.

There is a stunned silence. Then Mom begins to sniffle. "It took me ages to find pink plankton for the icing!" she wails.

Dad puts a fin around her.

I swim as fast as I can for the door. I just want to get away. Once I get outside the restaurant, I shake my head in the cooler water, trying to get rid of every last bit of icing. Ralph and Joe swim out behind me.

"Are you okay?" Ralph asks.

"No, I'm not okay!" I yell. "I've had

enough. Enough of Mom! Enough of Dad! Enough of Rick! Enough of Donny! And enough of my goofy head and everyone laughing at it!"

Joe pats me on the shoulder with about six of his tentacles. "Come on, Harry, it's not that bad. It's bad, yes, but not really, truly, awfully, terribly, humongously baddy-bad, like it is for me. I mean, you've only got three fins, a tail, and a hammer to find clothes for. Have you ever gone shopping with your mom and tried to find a hoodie with thirty-eight arms? No, you haven't. So things are much worse for me."

I shrug off Joe's tentacles. "But at least you only need one helmet. I've had enough! Lone sharks like Gregor the Gnasher have the right idea. They don't put up with moms and dads and double pink crash helmets and double-double pink cakes! No, they live in the open sea by themselves and do their own thing. No one bothers them, and they have a wonderful life!"

"But you're not a lone shark," says Ralph. "You're a hammerhead!"

That's when I have a brain wave. I look at him and start to smile, and my icing lipstick slides into my mouth. "Not for much longer. Starting tomorrow, I'm going to become a lone shark. I'm going to leave Shark Point for good and I'm going to go out into the ocean, and no one will ever be able to laugh at me again!"

CHAPTER 2

I'm swimming through the wide-open sea. I'm big, I'm brave, and I'm just like a great white. Not just any great white, though. I'm just like Gregor the Gnasher.

And just like Gregor, I'm leaving Shark Point behind, with cameras flashing and fish cheering my bravery.

"*Hurray! Hurray! Hurray!*" they shout as I swim and swim.

"*Hurray! Hum! Hurray! Hum! Hum! Hum!*"

I frown and stop swimming. Why are they saying "hum"? What's going on?

Oh.

I'm dreaming.

And the buzzing is Humphrey, my humming-fish alarm clock, trying to wake me.

I open one eye.

Humphrey pulls at my fin. "Come on, Harry, I've been humming for ages. If you didn't want to get up this early,

why did you tell me to wake you up now?"

I open my other eye but have to squint because Lenny, my lantern fish, is shining directly into it. "Come on, Harry!"

Lenny flashes on and off. "Time to rise and shine!"

I'm about to sigh when suddenly I remember.

Yes!

Today is the day I become a lone shark.

I launch myself out of bed and swim around the bedroom in my pajamas, looking in my drawers and under my bed for my cool Gregor the Gnasher T-shirt. When I've found it, I look at the list I made last night of things I need to take with me and start packing my back-pack. I can't wait!

LIST OF THINGS I NEED
TO BE A LONE SHARK

1. Gregor the Gnasher's autobiography. *Wrestling with Fame.*
2. Two packs of kelp krispies.
3. Uh... ???   ???

"Harry! What are you doing?" Humphrey says, jumping out of my way as I swim around the room.

"I'm trying to pack," I say.

"But why are you trying to pack?" asks Lenny, with a concerned look on his face. "And why are you getting up before your mom and dad? You never get up before your mom and dad. Shall I go and—"

"No!" I zip to the door, slamming it shut and barring it with my fins. "No, I don't want you to wake them up, they'll only try to stop me."

Humphrey frowns at me. "Stop you from doing what?"

I put on my most serious face and say, "I'm leaving," as dramatically as I can.

Humphrey and Lenny both start to smile.

"Oh," says Lenny. "I thought it was something important. But you're just having one of your tantrums about being a hammerhead.

You'll be back by dinner. You always are."

"Not this time," I say. "This time, I'm going for good. You just watch."

Lenny and Humphrey laugh, and Humphrey winks at me. "Yeah, right. So, what time do you want us to wake you up tomorrow? You'll probably want a nice long sleep after all the huffing you're going to do today!"

Humphrey and Lenny chuckle and high-fin each other.

I glare at both of them and zip up my backpack. "You can *try* to wake me up anytime you like. Because I won't

be here!" I swim over to the window.

"See you later, then!" Humphrey calls as I swim away from the house. *I'll show them,* I think. *I can be a lone shark. No problem.*

The streetlights are still on, casting orange pools of light on the coral pavement. In the distance, I can hear the odd whale-truck rumbling through the morning water, and beyond that I catch the sound of the first turtle bus from Shark Point rolling out to Crabton.

Shark Point seems so calm and peaceful. So quiet and—

"Haaaaaaaaarrrrrrrryyyyyyy!"

I leap up through the water in shock and turn to see Ralph and Joe speeding toward me. "Harry! Harry! Stop! Wait for us!" Ralph cries.

I shake my head and sigh. Honestly! How can you be a lone shark if no one will leave you alone?

"I was right, wasn't I?" Ralph says to Joe as they catch up with me. "I knew he'd get out early and try to give us the slip. Humphrey and Lenny were right—he *is* having a tantrum."

"*I am not having a tantrum!*" I shout.

Joe's bottom toots a couple of times

because he's a bit scared of shouting, and I hold up my fins.

"Look, I'm sorry. But I'm not having a tantrum this time, okay? I'm really doing this. I've packed, and I'm ready to head out into the open ocean to live the life of a lone shark."

"Show him the list," Ralph says, nudging Joe.

Joe nods and starts fiddling around with his tentacles. "I know it's here somewhere."

"Joe's been up all night, writing a list for you, haven't you, Joe?"

"Really?" I can't help being interested. I *love* lists.

Joe is still looking but manages a quick nod before turning a bit blue, then slightly purple, then completely green with embarrassment.

"This list," says Ralph, "shows you exactly why you shouldn't leave Shark Point. Right, Joe?"

Again, Joe turns, turns a little more green, and keeps looking. "Um . . . ," he says.

"This list has not two, not twenty,

not two hundred, but—count 'em—two hundred and forty-seven things on it that might go wrong for you out there!" Ralph announces. "Show him, Joe."

"Ummmmm."

Ralph frowns at him. "Come on, we're waiting."

"Ummmmm. . . ."

Ralph swims right up to Joe's ear and hisses, "Where's the list?"

"Ummmm." Bottom toot. Bottom toot. Bottom toot, toot, toot. "I think I've left it in my bedroom."

Ralph shakes his head. "Okay, Harry, wait there—we're going back to get the list."

I shake my head. "Look, I know you mean well, but I'm not interested in your list, not even if it has twenty-four thousand things on it. I'm going and that's it."

"You'll get lost! That's number forty-six, I think. . . ." says Joe desperately.

"I want to get lost!" I yell. "I want to get so lost I never come back!"

Joe turns white with fear. "But . . . y-you might get eaten!"

"Number eighty-seven," Ralph says.

I glare at them. "I'm a *shark*. I'm the one that does the eating. That's the way it works!"

294

Ralph holds up his fin. "But . . . but . . . where will I get my breakfast? I'm a pilot fish! You're leaving me to starve!"

I groan, undo my backpack and give Ralph one box of kelp krispies. "They should keep you going for a few days, until you find another shark to be friends with."

"But . . . !" Ralph and Joe shout.

"No! I'm going, and that's that. Don't follow me. You know I can outswim you both."

And with that, I tail-kick off down the street, stuffing fins into my eyes to rub, rub, and rub away the tears.

The town is fully awake now. Fish and turtles are coming out of their coral houses, on their way to work or school. I decide to keep to the back roads in case anyone else is out looking for me. I really hated saying good-bye to Ralph

and Joe, but it was for the best—I have to get away from Shark Point.

At the edge of town the buildings start to thin out, and my tummy flutters as I see the dark water of the open sea. I have to admit, I'm getting a bit nervous myself at the thought of striking out into the deep.

"Hey, Harry! What are you doing? Why aren't you on your way to school?"

I turn around. It's Cora and Pearl, the dolphin twins, and they're swimming toward me. They're holding their aqua-phones and typing away on them as they go, probably telling everyone on Plaice-book where I am.

"Look, I don't care what you say. I'm going! And you won't persuade me to stay!"

"What are you talking about?" asks Cora.

Oh.

"You haven't seen Ralph and Joe? You don't know that I'm leaving?"

They both look at their aqua-phones. "Nothing about it on Plaicebook," says Pearl.

"Oh. Well, I'm leaving Shark Point," I say. "I'm going out into the open ocean and I'm going to be a lone shark. I know you'll think it's a silly idea, but—"

"No, we don't," says Cora.

"It's an awesome idea," says Pearl. "You are sooooooo brave!"

Cora and Pearl hold up their aqua-phones and take pictures of me.

"Really?" I say. "I mean, yes, of course. It is a very brave thing to do, but hey, I am a very brave shark."

Cora nods.

I glance toward the dark ocean, and suddenly it doesn't feel quite so scary. I flex my dorsal muscles and wink at Cora and Pearl. "Wish me luck!"

As Cora and Pearl cheer me on and take more photos, I kick away from Shark Point and into the deep.

CHAPTER 3

It was all right being brave for Cora and Pearl, but pretty soon they're out of sight, and the view back to Shark Point is getting hazier. After a while, when I look back, all I can see is the same dark wall of water that I can see in front of me. And when I look down, it's even worse.

301

The sandy seabed I'm used to soon
becomes huge boulders with deep, jagged cracks in them. Surrounding the
boulders are tall forests of coral, their
branches reaching spiky fingers high up
into the inky blue water above.

"I'm not going back," I say out loud.

I say it out loud because the water
here is so silent and it feels good to
hear a voice—even if it is my own
voice.

BOOM!!!

"What's that?" I yelp, spinning around.
But it's too dark. I can't see anything.

BOOM!!! BOOOM!!!

BOOOOOOOOOOOOOM!!!!!

I look down. Nothing. I look up. Still nothing, just the weak light of the sun 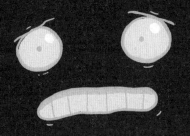 far above on the surface of the water.

"Hello?" I call out again, my voice sounding all high-pitched and girly. I'm not really expecting a reply, I just want to use my mouth to stop my teeth from chattering. So when I do get a reply, I almost turn inside out in fright.

"It's the whales breaching. Don't you know nothin'?"

I can't see who's speaking. "W-w-whales?" I stutter, trying to make my voice less girly.

"Yeah," says the voice, right in my ear. *BOOOOOOOM!!!!* (That's the whales, apparently.)

TOOT! (That's my backside.)

The voice snickers.

"Humpback whales. Every time they jump out of the sea for some air, they crash back into the water and it makes that booming noise. You really don't know nothin' about nothin', do you?"

"Who are you?" I ask.

"Who I am doesn't matter."

I turn quickly and catch a flash of silver in my eye. I twist right; then, at the last second, left, into a perfect inside-outy. There, in front of me, is a minnow. Small and silver, with a rounded nose and a dark black line running down the middle of his body.

"Oooh, you're quick, Hammerface," says the minnow with a laugh. And with a *swish!* he's gone.

"Head!" I shout at the empty water. "It's Hammer*head!*" I pull a fast turn, and the minnow is in view. He sticks out his tongue and—*swish!*—he's gone again.

"If it's all the same," says the minnow in my ear, "I'll stay behind you. From the size of you, you're a kid—but you could still have me for breakfast!"

"I'd eat you even if it wasn't breakfast time!" I growl.

"Like to see you try."

"Would you?"

"Yeah."

"You asked for it!" I yell and throw myself into a triple dorsal spin.

GNASH!

My teeth chomp down on empty water and I hear the minnow snickering. I turn my head slightly so that I can swivel one eye back and catch sight of him. He's lounging on his side, covering a yawn with a feathery fin. "Too slow, chum."

SWISH! and the minnow is gone. *Again.*

I stop myself from charging at him without thinking. That won't work—this minnow is way too slick for that. And I'm a lone shark now. Lone sharks use cunning and guile when they hunt. Gregor the Gnasher wouldn't be chasing around after a minnow like this without a plan.

Trouble is, I don't have a plan. I decide to switch on my hammer-vision. Hammerheads have the best senses of any of the shark species because their heads are so big. It's like having a load of extra eyes that can see through stuff. But what's gonna help me now is the tiny vibrations I'll be able to sense as the minnow moves.

PING!

There he is! Using my fin-tips and tail, I quickly calculate the best route to take to head the minnow off.

My mouth waters and I can practically taste the fresh fish.

Mmmmmmm. Yum!

I wind up my tail, tense my muscles, and kick down.

I race through the water at top speed, my tail flapping furiously.

PING!

PING!

PING! . . .

. . . *GNASH!*

My teeth chomp onto empty, cold, unfishy water.

"You're so slow, I could tie your fins into bows without getting eaten," he calls out from behind me. "You must be one hungry shark if this is the way you hunt!"

Swish! In a flash he's in front of me, winking. "Is that your stomach I can hear rumbling?"

It's true, my stomach is rumbling, and I hadn't realized just how hungry I am. I think of the box of kelp krispies in my backpack. I'd much prefer a tasty minnow but there's no way I'm going to be able to catch this one. He's far too

tricky. And there's no point sticking around here to be laughed at. I could have stayed in Shark Point for that. I turn and begin to swim away.

"Aw, don't you want to play no more?"

I shake my head and keep swimming.

"I can teach you how to hunt if you like?"

The nerve! A tiny prey fish like a minnow telling me how to hunt! But I don't give him the satisfaction of seeing how annoyed I am.

I say nothing and swim on.

"Suit yourself!" says the minnow, "but don't say I didn't offer." And with another lightning *swish!* of his silvery tail, the minnow is gone.

I swim on alone, getting more and more down in the dumps.

This is hopeless. Maybe Humphrey and Lenny were right. Maybe I will be home for dinner this evening, with my tail between my fins and a whole world of embarrassment to face up to.

Maybe I'm not cut out to be a lone shark after all.

Then I see something move out of the corner of my eye. It's a big something. A really big something. I look down at the seabed. I can make out boulders and coral forests, sharp branches sticking up in the gloomy half-light. Then . . .

There it is again!

A shadow, huge and slow moving, rippling over the rocks.

Because of the lack of sunlight, I can only just make out a dim shape. Maybe it's one of the humpback whales I heard booming earlier.

Or maybe it's something else . . . something with sharper teeth.

Gulp.

But . . . what's that? Is it a dorsal fin? Is it the . . . nose . . . the pointy nose of a shark? *A great white shark?*

Suddenly I'm more excited than scared.

Of course! I'm out in the deep—this is prime hunting water for great whites. Maybe . . . maybe. . . .

No, it can't be. . . .

Can it?

Could it be Gregor the Gnasher?!

I pull down my T-shirt and smooth out the picture of Gregor. Oh man, if it is Gregor, I'll be able to get his autograph. Better than that, maybe Gregor could teach me how to hunt. And then I'll show that minnow who the best hunter in the sea is!

Kicking my tail, I swim down and down toward the shape, smiling the biggest smile I've smiled since before my disaster of a birthday.

Faster and faster and faster. . . .

315

"Gregor! Gregor! Hey! Wait! I'm your number one fan!"

And that's when I see that the shadow isn't Gregor the Gnasher at all, but I'm swimming too fast to stop.

And I *really* need to stop—more than anything in the whole world. Because I'm swimming straight toward the open tentacles and fearsome gaping mouth of a giant squid!

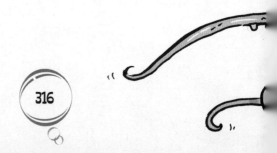

CHAPTER 4

I try everything I can to brake and change direction, but it's no good. I'm going way too fast.

And the giant squid really is *giant*!

It has about a million billion suckery arms, all twisting about in the water. Its

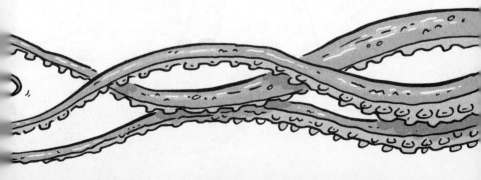

two big shiny black eyes, each as big as a turtle-kart, are staring right at me. And there, in the center of its huge, flat face, is the giant squid's mouth. It's deep, dark, and red, surrounded by a huge, razor-sharp beak!

How did I think this monster was Gregor the Gnasher?

The squid opens and shuts its beak really quickly, making a hissing sound like scissors cutting through sea-weed paper. He's showing me how deadly he is!

I push against the water hard with my fins. It takes all my strength to slow down even a little bit, and I could tail-flick myself for zooming down to the shadow without thinking of what could be lurking there. Oh, if only I'd listened to Joe and Ralph and stayed at home!

I push and push with my tail and feel myself start to slow. I look up to the dim surface of the ocean, many fathoms above. If only I could push harder, if only I could find the strength. . . .

"I promise I'll never try and be a lone shark again!" I whisper as I kick and kick.

It's working. I'm starting to slow down. I might just pull this off!

But that's when the giant squid shoots out his longest and suckeriest tentacle and grabs me right around the middle.

Puk!

Puk!

Puk!

That's the sound of the suckers attaching themselves to my skin.

I wriggle and twist, push and kick, snap and crunch my teeth, but I'm stuck fast.

"Let me go! Please! Let me go!"

The giant squid sucks the suckers

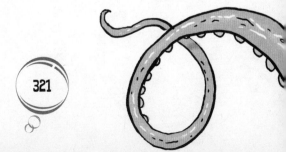

tighter and yanks me toward him, right up close to his hissing beak and huge, scary eyes.

"Let you go? Why would I let you go? I haven't had hammerhead in ages. Such a subtle flavor, the hammerhead. A reef shark or a great white can be tough and chewy, but a young hammerhead? Why, that's a taste to be savored, make no mistake!"

I gulp as the squid's mouth opens and closes and inside I see a thick purple tongue getting ready for some hammerheady flavors.

"I'm tough!" I yell, trying to break out

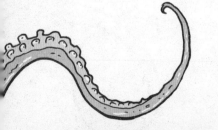

of the squid's grasp. "I'll stick in your throat. I'll give you indigestion! I'll make your breath smell!"

The squid hesitates for a moment. I think that maybe I've persuaded him not to eat me, but I'm wrong.

Another tentacle snaps out above my head, and I can see that it's holding a cookbook. Yet another tentacle starts to flip through the pages.

"Hmm, angelfish soufflé, crab cheesecake, grilled coral with a rack of sea squirt—that's a classic! Ah, here we are . . . hammerhead. Ooh, yes, that's just the ticket! Hammerhead Wellington with puffer fish pastry and a big splash of jellyfish gravy."

The squid sniffs up and down my body, making me shiver and shake, then

HAMMERHEAD WELLINGTON

licks his lips with his purple tongue. Ah, so fresh, so tasty, so alive . . . for now!"

I begin to struggle again, but all I'm doing is wearing myself out.

It's hopeless.

The squid gives a contented sigh as I go limp in his tentacles. "Ah, yes, so much better when lunch doesn't put up a fight."

Then he starts to swim down, carrying me like someone carrying their shopping home from the supermarket. I've never missed Shark Point so much in my life. I'm even missing Rick and Donny. What I wouldn't give right now to be wearing two pink crash helmets and to have Rick playing bongos on my hammer head. Anything would be better than this!

"Where are you taking me?"

"To my kitchen, of course," says the squid. "I need to cook you properly to make this meal the triumph I want it to be."

"Triumph? It's just lunch, isn't it?" I say sadly.

The squid stops dead in the water and looks at me. "Just lunch? Don't be silly, boy. Gordon Clamsey, Star Chef of the Seabed, doesn't do 'just lunch'! He creates menu masterpieces—he is an

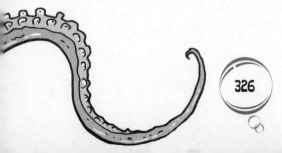

326

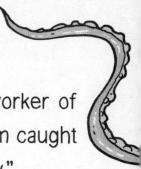

artist of the palate, a miracle worker of foodie wonder! You haven't been caught by just any old squid, you know."

I frown. "If you're a star chef, how come I've never heard of you?"

The squid shakes a few of his free tentacles in disgust. "It's not my fault those lame brains in Clam City aren't ready for a chef of my caliber in their hideous little restaurants. Thrown out just because I ate a few of the diners! I mean, what's a chef to do when he's a bit hungry and it's a slow day in the kitchen?"

"But a chef is supposed to feed the diners, not feed *on* them!"

"That's just what the restaurant owners said. Before I ate them."

My stomach flips over three times.

With a sniff and a ripple of his tentacles, Gordon Clamsey starts swimming down again. Soon the jagged boulder field that is the seafloor comes fully into view through the hazy blue water. Gordon pushes on toward a cave entrance. "Here we are, my boy!" he bellows. "Welcome to my kitchen, the place where the magic happens!"

As we squeeze through the narrow opening, he bangs my head against the roof.

"Ow!" I yell.

"Just tenderizing the meat!" Gordon booms, with a hearty laugh that makes my eyes wobble.

Inside the cave it's almost completely dark. It's also dead cold, and I shiver. As my eyes adjust to the light, I wish that it was completely dark. The cave floor is covered in bones. Fish bones, crab shells, and the jawbones of sharks. I see one huge jaw with a rack of teeth that can only have come from a great white, a great white who must have been as big as Gregor. If a shark like that can't escape from Gordon Clamsey, what chance does a wimpy hammerhead like me have?

None. *Gulp!*

Gordon pushes me up against the wall and ties me to a rock with thick, sticky strands of sea-weed.

Ugh! It's like being tied up with giant boogers!

Gordon swims back a little to admire his tentacle-work. He smiles and says, "Now, wait there. I'm off to get a few things to help you make my taste buds explode with delight. Stay fresh, now!" And with that Gordon leaves, and I'm all alone. Alone apart from the bones.

I jerk and strain in the cold, sticky grip of the seaweed but, like Gordon's suckered tentacles, it's far too strong for me to wiggle out of.

I think of how Rick and Donny would be killing themselves laughing if they knew how Harry the Lone Shark had found himself on Gordon Clamsey's menu as soon as he'd left town.

What about Joe and Ralph? How would they feel? They tried every-thing to make me stay and I didn't lis-ten. They'll probably blame themselves. And Mom and Dad? Oh, man! Now I feel really bad. Especially when I think of how mean I was about my birthday cake. I feel so ashamed.

I have to get out of here.

I try shouting "Help!" a few times. But

the cave is probably too deep down. And if the locals know there is a huge killer squid chef living in a cave of bones, I hardly think any of them will try to rescue me.

I try to calm down a bit, but I can't get the thought of that huge, scissory, squiddy beak coming toward me out of my hammer head! I bite my lip. What should I do? What should I DO??????????

PING!

PING!

Huh? Why is my hammer-vision suddenly going off?

333

PING!

It's picking up movement outside the cave. Gordon must be coming back!

"Typical!" I groan. "Hammer-vision is supposed to show me the things *I* want to eat, not show me the things that are coming to eat me!"

I close my eyes as it gets even closer.

PING!

PING!!

PING!!!

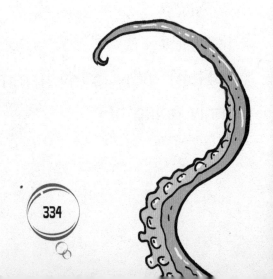

CHAPTER 5

"Yikes! You're in a pickle, aren'tcha?"

What?

I open one of my screwed-up eyes.

"What's up?" says the minnow. "You got time for a chat, or are you a bit tied up right now?" The minnow laughs his head off at his joke, even though

it's bad enough to be one of Dad's.

Then he comes up close to my face. "Thought it was you. I heard you yelling for help. You're not that brave for a lone shark, are you?"

I'm so pleased to see someone who isn't going to eat me that I don't care that the minnow's being mean.

"Get this stuff off me," I say.

The minnow looks at the sticky, boogerlike seaweed and makes a face. "You think I'm touching that? It looks like the squid sneezed on you."

"Please," I say, making my hammer-heady eyes as big and as appealing as I can. "You can nibble through it and I'll be free!"

The minnow shakes his head. "Listen, pal, there are two reasons I'm not going to get you out of that stuff. One, it looks like squid snot, and two, what's to stop you from eating me if I let you out, huh?"

"I promise I won't eat you."

"That's just what that fat great white, Gregor the Gnasher, said to my cousin Monty."

"Really?"

"Yep. Just before he ate him."

"Oh. Look, I don't know your name, and I'm sorry I tried to eat you before, but please help me. I promise I'm not like Gregor the Gnasher."

The minnow isn't listening. "See, if you don't wanna get caught by a giant squid, what you don't do is swim straight at one."

"I didn't know it was a giant squid!"

"Classic errors all the way, pal. Out in the open ocean? All alone? Error. Not really knowing what you're doing? Massive schoolshark error. Not even fast enough to overtake a minnow like me? Asking for major, error-y trouble, my friend. . . ."

"How does telling me that now help?"

The minnow nods his head. "Good point. Oh well, must be off. Places to be, sharks to annoy. . . ."

"Wait!"

"Why?" The minnow frowns at me. "We've pretty much covered everything. You're squid food and I'm off to have fun and *not* get eaten."

"Wait!" I plead. "If you won't get me out, please can you go to Shark Point and find my best friends Ralph and Joe? They'll come and rescue me!"

The minnow thinks for a moment. "And what's to stop this Ralph and Joe from eating me then, huh?"

"They're not sharks!" I say triumphantly, sure this will persuade the minnow.

"What are they, then?"

"Well, Ralph's a pilot fish and Joe's a jellyfish."

The minnow makes a disgusted face. "*Eeew!* Being a pilot fish has got to be

340

the worst job in the world. You wouldn't catch me eating stuff out of sharks' mouths!"

"Please! Will you go?"

But before the minnow has a chance to answer, we're startled by a suckery sound from outside the cave.

"It's hammerhead Wellington time!" calls Gordon's booming voice.

Swish!

The minnow vanishes.

Looks like I'm on my own.

Gordon enters the cave and grins. He waves a few tentacles around, bows as if he's in front of an audience, and holds up two shopping bags.

"You need three things to be a successful chef," says Gordon to the cave.

I look around to see if there are any

other squid who've come along to watch, but there aren't any. Perhaps Gordon just *thinks* he's talking to lots of other squid. I shiver some more. Being in the clutches of a killer chef is bad enough, but I'm in the clutches of a killer chef who's completely bonkers!

"First," continues Gordon, "you need the finest ingredients known to chef-kind!" Gordon empties the bags on the cave floor. I can see packets of dried jellyfish, bags of Piranha Puffs, and all kinds of weeds and spices. "Second, you need a kitchen worthy of your ingredients!" Gordon's tentacles shoot out in all

directions, and from the dark corners of the cave he drags a fancy captain's table (complete with red-checked table-cloth), a Coral and Limestone cooking stove connected to a sea gas canister, a huge number of shiny cooking utensils and, last, a clutch of sharp, evil knives.

I really don't like the way the blades glint in my ever-more-goggly eyes.

"And finally," bellows Gordon, throwing his tentacles wide, "the thing you need most of all is . . ."

I take a deep breath, terrified of what that last thing might be and how

it might be used to chop me into tiny pieces of shark sushi, or blend me into hammerhead-fin soup.

"The right hat!"

Huh?

Reaching up into the dark ceiling of the cave with two of his tentacles, Gordon brings down a huge white chef's hat. I look at it closely and see that it has been stitched together from several wrecked-ships' sails.

Gordon places the chef's hat on his head, like a mer-king putting on a crown. The puffy, mushroom-shaped top of the hat settles down and Gordon strikes a

pose, folding his tentacles one over the other over the other over the other over the other over the other over the other over the other over the other.

"And now," Gordon whispers, "we can begin!"

I try to push myself into the rock as Gordon picks up *one!*, *two!!*, *three!!!*, *four!!!!* of his sharpest knives and slowly makes his way toward me, licking at his razor-sharp beak with his leathery purple tongue.

CHAPTER 6

"*Wait!*" I scream as Gordon gets closer. "Wait! You've forgotten something really important!"

"No, I haven't," says Gordon, unconvinced. He looks around. "Ingredients. Check. Cooking stove. Check. Knives. Check, check, check, and check. Huge, floppy chef's hat. Check! Table. Check. Tablecloth. Checked. What else can I possibly need?"

Think of something! I say to myself. "You don't have . . ." *Come on!!! Come on!!!*

Then I have a brain wave. On all the cooking programs Mom watches, they're always going on about some- thing called seasoning.

"You don't have the right seasoning!" I say with a gasp.

Gordon's chef's hat has fallen over the tops of his eyes. He pushes it back, scratches at his forehead with three spare tentacles, and peers at me. "I've got all the seasoning I need right here."

"No, you haven't!"

Gordon pushes his hat so far back that it falls off. He scrabbles around on the floor, picks it up, and puts it back on his head. "Look, you, zip it. Food should not answer back. Now, back to the matter at tentacle. . . ."

"Honestly, you don't have the right seasoning—for hammerheads you need . . ."

Think. Think. THINK! Yes!

". . . you need pink plankton. That's the best thing for hammerheads." I remember how it had taken Mom ages to find pink plankton for the icing on the top of my birthday cake. If I can convince Gordon to go looking for some, it might buy me some time. . . .

"Pink plankton?" Gordon eyes me suspiciously. "I've never heard anything about hammerheads and pink plankton before."

"It's true," I say. "I saw it on . . ."

THINK! What's that program Mom watches? ". . . Musselchef. Honestly, if you don't have pink plankton, I am going to taste really boring. And I wouldn't want to see a brilliant chef like you make such a huge mistake."

"Well. . . ."

Yes. Yes. Come on.

"All right."

SCORE!

Gordon sighs. "I'll go and find some, but when I come back, you're going in the pan and I am frying you up for lunch and then having leftover hammerhead sandwiches for later. Is that clear?"

"Yes! Yes, it is!" I have to stop myself from cheering.

Still clutching the knives, Gordon turns around and swims out of the cave, grumbling to himself.

I know that this is my very last chance. If I don't get away now . . . I shiver at the horrible thought of being a giant squid's lunch (and dinner!).

The seaweed's too strong for me to get out of on my own, so if I'm going to get free, I'll have to find something that will help. *Okay. Concentrate. Find something. Anything* to get me out of this mess.

I look around. Because I'm tied to this dopey rock, my nose and fins can't reach any of the knives and utensils Gordon has left out on the table. I can't bend my neck to get my teeth working on the icky seaweed, either.

So what's left?

I look down and see that my tail is free. Great. That will be really helpful. Not.

But then . . .

I look beyond my tail to the floor of the cave. It's covered in bones and teeth and fish jaws. What if . . . ?

I *ping* on my hammer-vision and start scanning the cave floor. Look. Look. *Look!* Yes! There! Just in reach!

I start moving my tail. I swish it as hard and as fast as I can over the small patch of cave floor below me. Soon a huge cloud of sand and silt is rising into

the water. As I dangle, I'm uncovering more and more bones, and then, as the sand clears, I can see the edge of the cuttlefish bone I'd detected with my hammer-vision.

Cuttlefish bones are *razor*-sharp.

I push as hard against the seaweed as I can and wriggle my tail down a tiiiiiiiiiiiiiiiiiiny bit more. The tip of my tail just brushes the top of the exposed cuttlefish bone. That's a start!

I take a deep breath and squiggle down as hard and as far as I can. The bonds shift a little, and I can just . . .

YES!

My tail finally squirms under the cuttlefish bone and I flip it up.

The bone spins lazily into the water on a cloud of sand.

I reach out with my left fin.

Missed!

I lunge with my right fin.

Missed again!

The bone is still going up. I kick and kick, forcing myself against the snotty seaweed, and open my mouth to . . .

Chomp!

The cuttlefish bone is in my mouth. Luckily, not sharp-side up.

YES!

I tilt my head down to work on the seaweed.

The edge of the cuttlefish bone cuts through the sticky seaweed like a swordfish through sea-cow butter.

With a shake of my shoulders and a half-piked tail flip, I'm free of the snotty weed!

I shake the last pieces of seaweed

from my fins and kick away toward the entrance of the cave, and out into the dark water.

I've made it! I'm free!

Ping!

NO!

Ping!

NO!!

PING!!!

NO!!!!

My hammer-vision picks up a huge shape swimming toward me. A huge giant squid shape. Gordon Clamsey is back!

I thrust myself forward into

the water, back toward Shark Point, but I can feel from the currents in the water that he's getting closer.

"You tricked me!" Gordon shouts. 'You don't season hammerheads with pink plankton!"

"You don't?" I call back, swimming as fast as I can.

"No, and you know very well that you don't. I went to the library and got a kid-squid to look it up for me on the Interwet. And now," booms Gordon, "it's definitely *time for lunch!*"

"No. It's. Not!" I yell, swimming sharply from side to side to try and trick him.

"Oh. Yes. It. Is!"

Puk! One of Gordon's tentacles attaches itself to my back.

He starts to roll me toward his mouth.

"And I don't think I'll bother with the cooking," he says. "Sometimes food tastes best when it's RAW!"

I'm completely out of ideas. I'd set out to be a lone shark and ended up becoming a lunch shark. I close my eyes and hope it's over quickly.

"And what do you think you're doing with my little starfish?"

Mom?

361

I open my eyes. Gordon jumps in shock and lets me drop. I can't believe what I'm seeing either. There in front of us are Mom, Dad, Ralph, Joe, and a team of police sharks. A group of lantern fish are swimming in front of them, lighting the way. And in front of everyone is the minnow. He'd gone to get them after all!

"Mom! Dad! Ralph, Joe, and . . .
umm . . . what *is* your name?"

The minnow looks sheep-
ish. "It's not important,
okay?"

Mom is advancing on
Gordon. "I asked you

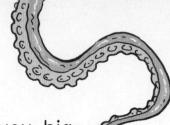

what you were doing, you big tentacled oaf!"

"Yes, what's going on here, sir?" one of the police sharks says, swimming over.

Gordon shrinks away from him. "Just having a bit of lunch, Officer. . . ."

"Having MY boy as a bit of lunch?" Mom swipes at Gordon with her tail. Gordon leans back farther.

"Do you know who my husband is?" Dad gives Gordon a little wave.

"He's the mayor of Shark Point. Do you think it's a good idea for you to be eating the son of the mayor?"

Gordon shakes his head.

"It really isn't a good idea, sir," the police shark says. He clinks his pair of giant-size tentacle cuffs threateningly.

"We've heard all about you from this brave little minnow," Mom says. "The police know all about your job in Clam City, and we know why you were thrown out of that restaurant. So I suggest you take my son off the menu or you'll have me, Mayor Hugo, and

every *shark* *in* *Shark* *Point* coming to turn you into *calamari*! Do I make myself clear?"

I can't believe what I'm seeing. Mom is scarier than Gregor the Gnasher!

Gordon nods and tries to hide his chef's hat behind his back. His tentacles start putting the knives inside his chef's jacket all on their own.

"Come on, Harry," says Mom. "It's time to go back home!"

I really don't mind being cuddled by Mom and Dad on the way back to Shark Point, even if it is in front of Ralph and Joe and my newest friend, the minnow. Mom insisted he come back to Shark Point for refreshments so she could say thank you.

As we approach the shallows around Shark Point, I turn to the minnow. "Listen, now that we're friends, you have to tell me your name. I can't keep calling you 'the minnow,' can I? It's silly."

"Not as silly as my name," the minnow says sadly. "You'll laugh at me."

"No, I won't," I promise. "How can I laugh at someone who's as fast and as clever and as brave as you? You're really cool."

"Not with a name like Marmaduke."

"Marmaduke?"

Marmaduke the Minnow nods.

I try not to laugh, but the bubbles from my nose show I'm swallowing a giggle.

Marmaduke frowns. "See, I told you you'd laugh! Well, I may have a silly name, but at least I don't have a head shaped like a novelty can opener."

I start to laugh out loud. Then Marmaduke does too. Then everyone laughs, except for Joe, who is being very, very quiet.

"What's up?" I ask him.

"My list of reasons not to leave Shark Point. It was garbage."

"Your list wasn't garbage," I say to him. "No way. It had two hundred and forty-seven things on it!"

"Yes, but none of those things was 'You'll get kidnapped by a crazy giant-squid chef'. That should have been in the top ten at least," Joe moans.

I laugh and pat Joe's jelly shoulder.

"Don't be sad. I'm just happy I've got such a brilliant friend who'd make a list that long to try to get me to stay. Shows me how lucky I *really* am!"

Joe smiles.

"So, do you still want to be a lone shark, Harry?" Dad asks as we swim into Shark Point.

I shake my head. "No way! The open ocean is way too dangerous for a hammerhead to be on his own. Especially one who tastes as nice as me!"

THE END

The Boy Who Cried Shark

CHAPTER 1

Zoooooooooooooooooooooooooooooooom!

Out of my room . . .

Screeeeeeeeeeeeeeeeeeeeeeeech!

Down the stairs . . .

Ziiiiiiiiiiiiiiiiiiiiiiiiiiiiiiiiiiiiiiiiiiiiiiiiiiiiiingg!

Into the hall . . .

YOOOOOOOOOOOOOOOOWLLLL!!!

"Sorry, Puddles!" I call back as I crash into our moth-eared catfish, sending him spinning out of control and bouncing into the wall. I don't stop to find out if he's all right. I must get to the jellyfishion before Mom and Dad!

It's Saturday night, and if I don't get there RIGHT NOW, they'll put on the news or some terrible sappy movie. They've been washing the dishes while I've been cleaning my room. There's always a rush to get to the den first after dinner, but tonight I *have* to get there first. So, instead of doing a total cleanup, I used my tail to sweep the mess under my bed. If Mom doesn't look too closely, I might just get away with it.

I come to the end of the hall, hook my dorsal on the doorframe, spin sideways (so my goofy hammery head doesn't get stuck in the door), and then—WHAM!— I'm in the den. Before Mom and Dad. YES!

Sailing around tail first, I slide into the finchair closest to the flat-screen jellyfishion and reach out with the flukes on my tail to flick the remote control off the coffee table and—

CLICK!

—down on the on button.

With a shiver and a fizz, the jellyfishion comes to life and I left-hammer the three button, just in time to see the judges for *The Shark Factor* being introduced. Pumping music blares and lasers burst across the stage, lighting the huge undersea set. The announcer, with his big, booming whale-size voice, waits for the pumping music to stop and then shouts out the names of the judges as they appear.

"Paddy!"

That's Paddy Snapper, the saltwater crocodile from Emerald Island. He slithers down the ramp on his yellow belly.

"Ellie!"

That's Ellie Electra, the smooth-bodied electric eel with ultra-shiny skin. She shimmies down the ramp and wraps herself around Paddy.

"Bobby!"

That's Bobby Barnacle, who is so tiny, he slides down the ramp under his own

personal magnifying glass so that everyone can see him.

"Marcus!"

And lastly, it's Marcus Sea-cow, wearing his trademark leather pants. He
waves his pink tail at the audience, and

with ocean-size smiles the four judges float to their huge clamshell seats.

"Oh no. Not this."

I look around at the sound of Dad's voice. He and Mom are swimming in from the kitchen. I grip the remote control tightly.

"I was hoping to catch some of my interview on the news," Dad says. Dad is mayor of Shark Point, and there's nothing he likes better than seeing himself on jellyfishion.

Mom flops down on to the sea-sponge sofa and groans. "Harry, do we have to watch this trash?"

Most weeks I wouldn't have minded. I mean, there are only so many times you can watch a fish being told he sings like a ship's horn that's got a seagull stuck in it. But this week . . . oh, man . . . this week I *have* to see the special guest who's opening the show.

380

We've been talking about it all week at school. Me, Ralph (my pilot-fish friend) and Joe (my jellyfish pal) have been finding it really difficult to concentrate in class. In the end, our teachers had to ban anyone from even mentioning *The Shark Factor.*

"But, Mom," I say, "I *have* to watch it tonight."

"Why?" she says, looking puzzled.

I let out a massive sigh. "Seriously, Mom, if you were any more uncool, we'd have to stick you on an iceberg. Gregor the Gnasher is singing his *first ever* single tonight."

My stomach is doing little flips just thinking about it. Gregor the Gnasher is a great white shark and my number-one hero. Not only is he the Underwater Wrestling Champion of the World (signature move: the fin-chop with tail-driver), he's also an action-movie star and now he's breaking into the music business as a rapper called G-White.

Tonight's performance has been the talk of the interwet, and the number of 'GREGOR' fan pages on Plaicebook has tripled in two days—making the system crash.

Marcus Sea-cow floats up from behind his desk.

"Ladies and gentlefish, welcome to *The Shark Factor*!"

The crowd goes wild.

Marcus Sea-cow grins and gestures to the stage. "And now, opening the show with his debut single, 'Bite It,' please welcome the one, the only, Geeeeeeeeeee-White!"

Horns ring out across the stage. Then comes the beat of drums. Search-lights start flashing through the water. A huge, glittery curtain opens at the back of the stage and

there's Gregor, floating fin-high on a column of bubbles. Two dolphins wearing shiny dresses are dancing on either side of him. Around his neck is a big gold shark's tooth, hanging on a gold chain that's so thick, it looks as

if it came from the anchor of a cruise ship. He's wearing a red Shike track-suit with diamond-encrusted sneakers on each fluke of his tail.

Oh, man!

The audience has gone crazy. I sneak my tail toward the remote to turn the volume up. Sea-cow, Barnacle, Electra, and Snapper float up above their judges' desk and start clapping along.

G-White nods to the beat as the dolphins sway beside him.

"I've got a big bite cuz I'm a great white," he raps.

I have to put my fin across my mouth to stop myself from squealing like a girl-shark.

"Great white!" the audience shouts back to him.

G-White grins, showing every single one of his three thousand and seventeen teeth. "I love causing FRIGHT, cuz I'm a great white!"

"Great white!" I join in with the audience.

"He's not too bright, he's a goofy great white," Dad mutters.

Huh?

I turn around and glare at Dad. He's shaking his head as he looks at the screen.

"Well, look at him," Dad says. "He might have lots of teeth, but I bet he couldn't think his way out of a wet paper bag."

"Dad!"

"Oh, come on, Harry. It's not exactly poetry, is it?" Dad says. "In my day we had real singers. Fish like Sting Ray and Sealion Dion. Now she could reach those high notes. This fool couldn't pitch a tent, let alone a tune."

Now Mom's shaking her head too. "I really don't know what anyone sees in that ridiculous big tooth-head. He's all teeth and no pants."

I can feel myself getting *really* angry

now. I've been looking forward to this all week, and now they're ruining it. "Be quiet!" I hiss. "I want to hear the chorus."

But they won't clam up.

"*Bite it*? Is that all he can sing about? Being mean? I don't think that's a very good example to be setting for the youngsters of Shark Point," Dad says in his "serious" voice.

"He's not mean!" I protest. "Not really."

"Gulp in ONE BITE, cuz I'm a great white!" screams G-White from the jelly-fishion.

Mom and Dad just look at me.

I'm torn. I just want to listen to the song, but I feel like I have to defend Gregor. He is my hero after all. I want to be like him. Even if the only thing I could gulp with one bite is a minnow. Actually, I couldn't even manage that

389

when I met Marmaduke the Minnow, my new friend. That doesn't matter, I tell myself. I have to convince Mom and Dad that G-White is a good shark now.

I open my mouth to continue the argument, but Mom holds up her fin.

"Not another word, Harry," says Mom. "I think we should turn to another channel; I'm really not happy about you watching this. Great whites shouldn't even be allowed on jellyfishion, the way they frighten communities. It's a disgrace."

"But Gregor isn't like that anymore,

Mom. He hasn't eaten anyone for two years, seven months, and eleven days!"

"No, Harry. I'm sorry," Mom grabs the remote from my fin and flicks the jelly-fishion channel.

"Oh, Hubert."

"Oh, Gloria."

Oh no! It's *Drownton Abbey*! Two terribly fancy crabs are having a terribly fancy conversation, while doing some terribly fancy kissing, in the terribly fancy drawing room of a TERRIBLY TERRIBLE COSTUME DRAMA!

"Mom, it's just an act! Gregor isn't scary. He just pretends to be!"

"Well," Dad says, "he's scaring us by polluting the waves with his awful noise."

I can tell that they're not going to let me see the rest of the performance. The thing I've been waiting for the whole entire week is ruined.

"You two just don't understand!"

I swim up from the chair and swish out of the den, slamming the door behind me. I go straight to my room and throw myself onto the bed.

"It's not fair!" I shout, with a couple of prickly tears in my eyes trying hard to get out. I wipe them away with the tips of my fins. Then I beat my fins on the bed.

Barrap! Barrap! they go as they hit the seaweed blanket.

Hmmm.

Actually, that's not a bad beat.

Barrap, barrap.

Thud. Thud. Swish! goes my tail.

That rhythm's pretty good, I think to myself. Suddenly, I feel a little bit better. Maybe I've discovered a cool new talent. Maybe I'm not so different from G-White after all. I mean, he's a huge great white wrestling, movie, and singing star, and I'm just a little nobody hammerhead, but what if I can rap too?

Barrap! Barrap! go my fins.

Swish. Thud. Thud! goes my tail.

"I'm a hammerrrrrrrrrrrhead. And that's a bit bad actuallyyyyyy," I rap.

It didn't even rhyme.

I try again. A little faster on the bar-raps this time.

"H-h-h-h-hammerhead. I'm kinda blue if you look at me in the right light, and sometimes nearly red."

No, I'm not. I'm never red. That's just really silly.

I need something better that rhymes with hammerhead.

Lots of cool things rhyme with great white. That's why G-White's rap sounded so good. I have to think. . . .

"Hammerhead . . . hammerhead . . . sounds just like jam and sea-bread."

That is clearly the worst rap in the history of the world. Ever.

And then I hear someone laughing.

395

I look up from the bed, and see Larry, my lantern-fish night-light, and Humphrey, my humming-fish alarm clock. They're both rolling on the floor, clutching their sides and giggling like crazy at my dorky attempts to rap like G-White.

"Stop laughing!" I yell.

Larry looks at me, his lantern flashing on and off as he chuckles. "You mean you weren't trying to be funny?"

"No!"

"Are you sure?" asks Humphrey, buzzing away happily.

"Yes!"

Larry and Humphrey help each other off the floor, both trying—and failing—not to laugh.

"Be quiet, you two!" I shout, pulling the seaweed blanket over my hammer. "I'm trying to sleep."

But I can still hear them giggling

as they swim back to the shelf above my bed. Great. I bet G-White's alarm clock and lamp don't ever laugh at him.

Sometimes it really stinks being a hammerhead shark. Sometimes it's even worse. And then there are days like today, when just about everything goes wrong and it's worse than worse can be. As I drift off to sleep, I hope that some day I'll finally get to meet Gregor the Gnasher. If I met Gregor, he could show me how to wrestle, or act, or rap. . . .

Then no one would laugh at me.

I bet he could teach me stuff that
would blow Larry and Humphrey and my
mean parents out of the water!

But until then, I'm just going to be a
dull hammerhead—that NOTHING COOL
RHYMES WITH!

CHAPTER 2

In the morning I can't wait to get out of the house. Even though it's Sunday, and Sundays are usually boring in Shark Point. Mom and Dad don't even notice that I'm not talking to them over breakfast. They seem to have completely forgotten that they upset me last night.

Dad's writing a speech as his breakfast goes cold, and Mom keeps tickling
me behind my hammer and calling me
her "little starfish." I just stare into my
bowl of kelp krispies and bite my lip. I
bite it a bit too hard as Mom tickles me
again.

"Ouch!" I say.

No one notices.

Great.

I bet this doesn't happen in G-White's
house. I bet everyone notices the second he gets mad about something. I leave
my bowl on the table to show them how
angry I am. But Mom just picks it up and

puts it in the dishwasher without saying a thing.

It's like I don't exist!

I grab my jacket and head over to Ralph's. At least he'll be glad to see me.

Ralph lives in a block of coral apartments about five minutes swimming away from our house. But I get there even quicker than usual because:

1. It's Sunday so there's hardly any traffic on the roads.

2. I'm swimming extra fast because . . .

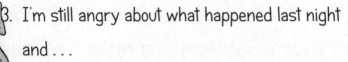

3. I'm still angry about what happened last night and . . .

4. I'm even angrier that at breakfast. Mom and Dad acted as if nothing happened.

Sometimes making a list helps me think more clearly and get my thoughts in order. This list doesn't. When I go over it again in my head, I feel even angrier and swim even faster.

I swish to a halt outside Ralph's bedroom window.

"Ralph!" I call. I wait a bit and the window opens. Ralph's head pokes out and he yawns.

"Morning," he says, rubbing his eyes and sliding slowly out of the window,

still in his pajamas. It isn't like Ralph to be so sleepy. He's usually raring to go in the mornings because he wants to get his breakfast out of my mouth. Pilot fish eat the leftovers from between sharks' teeth, and yes, it is as gross as it sounds. To be honest, I'd rather have a toothbrush, but then how would Ralph eat? So I open my mouth and wait.

Ralph yawns again, and quickly pokes around, pulling out a few half-eaten kelp krispies. He chews them slowly.

"What's up with you?" I ask.

"Late night," he says between little yawns. "I must have watched G-White about a hundred times on rewind. It was awesome, wasn't it?"

I start feeling angry about last night, so I try to change the subject as quickly as I can. "Yeah, awesome. So what should we do today?"

Ralph gives yet another yawn. "Sorry,

Harry. I've got homework to finish before tomorrow. I was supposed to do it last night, but I was too busy watching G-White. Mom says I have to do it today."

Great.

"Why don't you go and see what Joe's doing?" says Ralph, scratching his belly and swimming slowly back up to his bedroom window. "See you at lunchtime, okay?" He disappears inside without even waiting for a reply.

I'm furious.

We always get together on Sunday mornings. But now Ralph can't make it *because he stayed up too late watching G-White.*

I swim away in a huff, darting through town as fast as I can. By the time I get to Joe's family's cave I'm a little bit calmer, but not much.

I ring the bell and through the hanging fronds I see Joe float up to the entrance. He bumps into the wall and looks at me with bleary eyes.

"Yo!" he says slowly, with a yawn.

I can see exactly where this is going. "Up late watching *The Shark Factor*, right?" I ask.

Joe nods and his body changes

407

from yellow to light green, the color he always goes when he's really, really tired.

"Yeah, it was awesome, wasn't it? We watched it over and over again. Well, I was behind the sofa at the beginning because those explosions were a bit loud, but otherwise it was GREAT!" Joe sticks out his tentacles and scowls, in an

impression of G-White when he was floating on the column of bubbles. "I'm thinking of changing my name to Jel-Fish. What do you think?"

If I say anything, it will just be nasty, so instead I nod and try to put on a convincing smile.

Joe relaxes a few of his tentacles. "Yeah, I think it suits me too."

If I grit my teeth any harder, I think I might break them. "Are you coming out?" I manage to say.

Joe shakes his head. "Sorry, bro, Jel-Fish gotta stay in his crib and help the parental unit with the house."

"You mean your mom wants you to clean your bedroom?" I say.

"Truth."

I can't stay a second longer or I'll explode, so I wave good-bye and swim away in a double . . . no . . . *triple* huff.

It seems I'm the only person in Shark Point not to have seen the jellyfishion event of the year. All because my parents are the uncoolest parents in the ocean. As if it isn't bad enough having a head shaped like a hammer, now everyone will think I'm 100 percent more dorky because I didn't get to see G-White.

I swim down to the park, but it's

empty. Everyone's still in bed then. Great. I swim on.

It seems like the whole town is taking a long time to wake up and get going, even for a Sunday. The stores are deserted and I'm getting more and more bored. I'm getting so bored that I'd even be happy to see Rick Reef and Donny Dogfish, my two least favorite sharks. Even Donny snickering while Rick FLUBBERS my head would be better than this.

My tail is starting to ache and I realize I've been swimming around too fast for too long. I decide to rest for a bit. I'm by my

school now and I can see that the play-grounds are empty, so I swim down to the finball goalposts and lean back against the net.

I wonder what G-White is doing after his performance last night. Is he wandering around his hometown like Billy No-Friends feeling all down in the dumps? Of course he isn't. He's probably in his gold-plated hot spring, scrubbing his back with gold-plated scrubbing brushes while gold-plated pilot fish delicately pick the leftover caviar from between his gold-plated teeth.

Humph. I turn around and bury my hammer in the net.

"It's worse than being dead, being a ham-ham-hammer head," I whisper to myself. "I should've stayed in bed. I'm a ham-ham-hammerhead."

I flex my fins. I want to pound the ground with them.

"What kind of lyrics are they?" someone calls out from behind me.

Huh?

"They're, like, totally the worst lyrics EVAH!"

I flip around and see Cora and Pearl, the dolphin twins. They must have swum up behind me while I was trying out my latest useless rap.

Cora and Pearl strike poses. They look just like G-White's backup singers.

"If you wanna do lyrics right . . . , " says Pearl.

"You gotta sing about love," says Cora, and they high-fin each other.

"You gotta get smoochy-woochy." Pearl blows a kiss at Cora, who takes a picture of her on her SeaPhone.

"You gotta get lovey with the dovey." Cora puckers her lips and flutters her eyelashes as Pearl takes a picture of her. Pretty soon their camera-phones are flashing almost as much as the lights on *The Shark Factor* last night.

I think I'm going to be sick. I start to

swim away, but the camera flashes are following me.

"Don't you want us to help you, Harry?" says Cora as she swims alongside me.

I say nothing. I don't want to be mean. It's not their fault I didn't get to see G-White last night. I just want to be left on my own to sulk.

Pearl starts to rap while Cora drums her fins on her stomach. "Harry wants to sing, but he ain't got a thing. Bring it."

I swim out of the school grounds toward the Point, but the twins don't look like they're going to leave me alone.

They're having far too much fun rapping about me.

"Harry, don't run away—listen to what we say. Word."

Hopefully they'll leave me alone soon. I swim on like crazy, trying to get away from them. But Cora and Pearl swim after me, laughing and singing. I stick my fins in my ears, but I can still hear them.

I'm at the Point now. There's nowhere else to go except the deep ocean. If I just

ignore the twins, maybe they'll go away.

Or maybe they won't. Maybe today is going to be even worse than yesterday!

And then something catches my eye. Out in the dark wall of water beyond the Point I see a huge shadow.

I take my fins out of my ears.

"Don't look so sad; you're really not that bad."

"Yes, he is."

"I know—I just wanted a rhyme."

"Shhh!" I say. "Look!"

I point toward the shadow. It's big and getting bigger. I squint into the darkness.

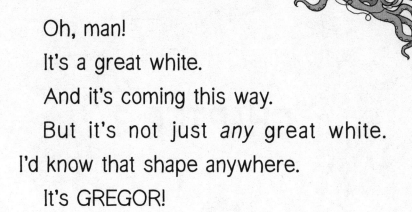

Oh, man!

It's a great white.

And it's coming this way.

But it's not just *any* great white.

I'd know that shape anywhere.

It's GREGOR!

CHAPTER 3

"It's a great white!" I yell.

But before I can say that I think it's Gregor, the twins start SCREAMING.

"We're under attack! We're under attack!"

CRASH!

That's Cara knocking into my left

hammer as they rush to get away.

"Wait!" I yell. My head is stinging and my stomach feels like a washing machine as I spin around and around. "He's not going to hurt you."

But it's too late. I manage to stop myself spinning and see the twins racing back toward town screaming, "We're all going to die! We're all going to die!"

I look back over my shoulder. Gregor is still moving toward me through the water. But I can't stay and talk to my hero.

I've got to find Pearl and Cora. I've got to stop them.

I try to use my hammer-vision to locate a fast-moving current to ride on. Dolphins and hammerheads are both fast swimmers, but Pearl and Cora have had a good head start and I'm still dizzy from all the spinning.

Unfortunately, it seems that the lazy Sunday feeling of the town has spread to the water, as the currents are all really slow. I'll just have to kick my tail as hard as I can.

My muscles are starting to cramp from all the swimming I've already done this morning. But I can't stop. I need to catch up with the twins. I kick even faster and feel myself surge through the ocean. I'm going almost as fast as Gregor! I can do this! I'm sure I can get to them before they cause any panic.

Or maybe not.

As I reach the main road, I see fish, sharks, and crabs coming out of their houses and stores. Some are still in their pajamas. Some little kids are crying, and their moms and dads are putting their fins around them.

"Have you seen them?" a squid calls to me as I zoom past.

"Seen what?"

"The school of great whites. The twins said they're about to attack Shark Point!"

Oh no! This is worse than I thought.

Panic is spreading through the town. A turtle bus coming in from the Crabton road has clearly tried to turn around and crashed into the side of a supermarket. It looks like all the passengers and the turtle are okay, but the coral wall of the supermarket has a huge hole in it, and loads of bags of piranha puffs are drifting out into the water.

I swim on.

In the distance I catch a glimpse of

Cora and Pearl as they reach Seahorse Square. If they've caused this amount of panic just going up the main road, who knows what's going to happen next!

I kick on, ignoring the pain in my tail and fins and the burning in my gills.

Cora and Pearl disappear around the corner. All I can hear is the buzz of conversation from the fish and sharks in the street. The number-one topic is "Shark alert!"

When I get to Seahorse Square, there's already a crowd gathering around Cora and Pearl. Fish, dolphins, crabs, and sharks. The dolphin twins are outside

the mayor's office, banging on the door.

"What's all this noise about?" a voice shouts from the other side of the square.

Oh no!

It's Dad. He's got his mayor's chain around his neck. He pushes through the crowds toward his office. Mom is swimming behind him and her face looks all concerned. I can see that she's looking for

me and she's really worried. I hold up my fin and wave to her, knowing exactly what's coming next.

Mom catches sight of me and her face lights up. "Angelfish! You're all right!"

"Yes, Mom, I'm fi—pshhhttttttthh!"

I'm trying to say that I'm fine, but she

swims across so fast and throws her fins around me so hard that my mouth is buried in her coat.

More and more fish are cramming into the square. Everyone seems terrified. I need to do something.

"I need to do something!" Dad says.

Huh?

He swims up above the crowd, waving his fins around.

"Citizens of Shark Point!"

Everyone ignores him and continues to panic.

"CITIZENS OF SHARK POINT!" Dad yells at the top of his gills.

Everyone still ignores him.

Mom lets me go. "WILL YOU ALL BE QUIET?!" she shouts. Silence falls.

Mom's using "the voice." It's the voice she uses to tell me off when I've been very bad. It's loud and it's scary. I hear a bottom tooting.

I look around, and see Joe blushing as he swims into the square. "Sorry!" he whispers.

He's followed by Ralph, Rick, and Donny.

It seems like the whole town is here. Rick takes a flubbery swipe at my hammer, but I manage to duck out of his way

and float nearer to Mom. He wouldn't dare to now, not when she's using "the voice."

"Citizens of Shark Point," Dad says again, a little calmer now. "We must not panic. We must be calm. We must not worry ourselves unnecessarily!"

"It's all right for you; you're a shark," a turtle calls from the crowd. "It's not you who's going to get eaten, is it?"

The shouting and the panicking start again. An old, ruddy-faced dolphin called Mr. Bottlenose brings Cora and Pearl forward. "Now, tell everyone what you saw, girls."

Cora trembles.

Pearl shakes.

"Well, w-w-w-we didn't really see anything," Cora stutters.

"H-H-H-H-Harry did," Pearl says, pointing at me.

It seems every eye in the square is now looking at me. I can feel my cheeks turning red.

"Oh, look, he's turning pink, just like a girl," Rick snickers to Donny.

Mr. Bottlenose swims up and looks at me. "Did you see great whites, boy?"

"Yes, but only—"

Before I have time to tell them the

rest, Mr. Bottlenose is spinning around, yelling, "It's true! It's true!"

"Um, if we could just calm down a bit," says Dad.

Mr. Bottlenose grabs my fin. "Take us

to them, boy," he bellows. "We've got to see what we're up against!"

With that, twelve strong dolphins come out of the crowd and follow as Mr. Bottlenose leads me back toward the edge of the Point. Mom and Dad swim after us.

"You've got to listen!" I plead, but Mr. Bottlenose waves me aside and swims on determinedly.

Ralph and Joe swim up beside me. "You had any lunch yet?" asks Ralph.

"Is that all you can think about?" I say.

"I'm starving! I hardly had any of

your kelp krispies earlier because I was so tired."

"Don't remind me," I say a bit grumpily. But I don't mind I missed *The Shark Factor* so much anymore, now that I know we're about to see Gregor in the flesh. And hopefully then everyone will calm down. Gregor is a superstar now— he's not going to eat *anyone*.

Eventually we get to the edge of the Point. Mr. Bottlenose pushes me forward. "Where are they, boy? Show us."

I flick on my hammer-vision and scan the dark water ahead. "Mr. Bottlenose, please, it's not—"

"No need to be scared, boy," Mr. Bottlenose interrupts. "Just show us where you saw them and we'll do the rest."

The strong dolphins are rolling up their shirtsleeves and getting ready for trouble.

PING!

My hammer-vision bursts into life and starts giving me information.

Gregor's still here! And he's coming toward us.

PING! Fifty feet and closing.

PING!!! Forty feet and closing.

"What can you sense, boy? Tell us!" Mr. Bottlenose yells.

435

"It's a great white, all right," I say. "And it's coming this way . . . but, Mr. Bottlenose, you must listen to me, it's only Gre—pshhhtttttthh."

That's Mom, pulling me into her coat again. "Don't worry, my little starfish. I'll protect you!"

"But li—pshhhttttthh! It's okay, we're not in any da—pshhhttttthh!"

I give up.

The strong dolphins have all formed a line on the edge of the Point, protecting the crowds of fish and sharks behind them. My hammer-vision is **PINGING** like crazy.

We can all see the shadow coming toward us out of the gloom. It's the biggest shark I've ever seen.

It must be Gregor. But then . . .

"Sea-flowers for sale, sea-flowers!

Who will buy my lover-ly sea-flowers?"

Huh?

Double "huh?"

TRIPLE "HUH?"!

Out of the gloom comes the shark. But it's *not* a great white.

It's a great big basking shark! She's wearing a long floral dress and a floppy fern hat, and carrying a huge bag of flowers. "Oh, who will buy my lover-ly sea-flowers? Bouquet of sea urchins? Vase of coral clusters?" she says.

The citizens of Shark Point aren't panicking anymore—they're laughing.

At me!

The basking shark can't stop grinning
as the relieved townsfish rush up to her
to buy her flowers.
FLUBBER!!!!
Rick boings my rubbery hammerhead

from behind. "Awesome hammer-vision, T-Bone face," he whispers in my jangling ear. "What's going to be next? Giant squids under all our beds?"

A new, horrible list starts writing itself in my mind.

1. I can't rap.
2. I'VE GOT A STUPID HEAD!
3. My hammer-vision isn't working properly anymore.

My hammer-vision was the ONLY cool thing about being a hammerhead. Now everyone thinks it doesn't work.

There are now exactly ZERO cool things about being a hammerhead shark.

ZERO cool things about being ME!

441

CHAPTER 4

Cora and Pearl aren't talking to me. They blame *me* for the panic *they* caused in town yesterday.

Rick and Donny snicker and whisper every time they swim past me in the school hall.

Joe and Ralph are trying to be nice,

but I can tell they're a little bit embarrassed to be friends with the 'kid who cried great white,' as everyone on the jellyfishion news last night was calling me. You would think that Mom and Dad would be trying to cheer me up, but no. They've been too busy trying to get Dad on jellyfishion so that he can tell everyone what a great mayor he was yesterday.

When I get to my desk in class, I see that someone has drawn a big bunch of flowers on it.

Great.

I'm never gonna live this down.

Luckily, the first lesson after assembly is PE with Mr. Skim, our flying-fish teacher, and there's going to be a cross-seabed swim. At least that gives me a chance to make the other kids remember that I'm a fast shark with a great sense of direction (when my hammer-vision is working properly, that is).

Mr. Skim is waiting for us on the field, doing fin-ups in his shiny track-suit. "Okay," he says, getting up as we file out of the locker rooms. "The route for today's cross-seabed swim is quite simple. From school you take the

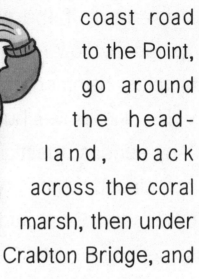

coast road to the Point, go around the head-land, back across the coral marsh, then under Crabton Bridge, and back to school. Any questions?"

My stomach sinks as Rick raises a fin. "Mr. Skim, what should we do if we see any vicious, dolphin-eating, urchin-chewing, crab-killing, fish-feasting FLOWER SHARKS on the swim?"

Everyone, including Ralph, thinks this

is hilarious. If the seabed could open up and swallow me right now, I'd be the happiest hammerhead alive.

Mr. Skim smiles but doesn't play along. "Any *serious* questions?"

Rick and Donny are high-finning each other, and Cora and Pearl are typing something on their SeaPhones. Probably putting Rick's joke up on Plaicebook.

Great.

Mr. Skim blows his whistle, and the swim is underway.

I kick away with my tail as fast as I can. Normally I would swim slower to be with Ralph and Joe—they're not as fast as me

and I don't like to leave them behind. But today, I just want to get my hammer down and swim as fast as I can. My face feels waaaaaaay red after Rick's joke, and the faster I go, the cooler the sea water is, taking the heat out of my cheeks.

I get to the Point in record time, just ahead of the leading pack. Rick's a very fast swimmer, but I think he's too busy fooling around with Donny and showing off to the dolphin twins to keep up with me today. I sneak a look behind me, and see him swimming on his back, blowing bubbles out of his gills at Cora and Pearl who are laughing their heads off.

I kick on.

Over the Point and on to . . .

Oh, blubber!

I can't remember which way Mr. Skim wanted us to go. Was it around the headland first, or down across the coral marsh? If Rick and the others see me going back to ask directions, I'll never hear the end of it. "Harry's had another hammer-vision epic fail!" I can almost see their Plaicebook status updates now.

I zoom down onto the coral marsh, convinced that I'm going in the right direction. I kick on and on, determined to get to the finish line first.

The water is getting warmer. I can feel it on my face.

Double blubber!

I should have taken more time to think about the route. It would have been the headland first, before the coral marsh, because from the Point, the coral marsh route will take me straight toward . . .

The shallows.

This is the one place that none of us are allowed to go, except accompanied by an adult. As the spongy coral marsh thins out, the seabed becomes sandy and shallow. The light becomes much brighter, and the water much warmer.

The chances of bumping into human beings, or leggy air-breathers as we call them, are really increased here.

But if I turn around, and go back the way I came, I'm going to be last in the cross-seabed swim.

I *can't* be last.

What should I do?

Then I have an idea. If I continue on, right across the shallows, there's a coral channel that doubles back and comes right out at the Crabton Bridge. If I go as fast as I can, I could use that instead of going around the headland, and still win the race.

Smart!

I swish my tail and start swimming at double speed.

The seabed is leveling out. The water is heating up like a lovely relaxing hot spring, and the sunlight glitters all around. It's a shame we don't get to go to the shallows very often, it's a really beautiful and welcoming place. . . .

PING!

Huh?

My emergency hammer-vision is kicking in at the first sign of danger. Up above me is a huge shadow blocking out the sun. Suddenly, I'm in a shaft of cold water, and I don't know if I'm shivering from the cold or from fear.

Probably both!

The shadow is big and black as it skims through the water. My hammer-vision is **PINGING** off the scale. I slam to a halt. There's only one thing that shadow can be.

A shark.

I listen to hear if it's selling flowers.

Nothing. No sound at all.

A huge shark cutting silently through the water can only be up to one thing.

Hunting.

And a shadow that big can only be from one kind of hunter.

A GREAT WHITE!

Now I'm torn.

Do I want to go on and win the race, or should I go back, get the others, and show them that I *do* know a great white when I see one?

Oh, man . . .

Okay. I can win a race ANYTIME, but this might be my only chance to show them that my hammer-vision *does* work!

I turn around, hurrying out of the shallows and back across the coral marsh.

I'm imagining the twins' Plaicebook updates once I prove to them that my hammer-vision works. . . .

I zoom out of the marsh and slam hard into Ralph and Joe, who are still slow-coaching their way down from the Point to the headland.

"Hey!" says Ralph.

Pop. Pop. Pop. Pop, says Joe's rear. "Watch it!" he manages to yell before his arms and fronds curl up into sea-horse tails in my wake.

"Shark!" I say breathlessly, pointing back over the coral marsh. "Shark!"

"Yeah, right, what's this one selling?

Dolls?" Rick has appeared with Donny behind Ralph and Joe.

"I don't have time to argue—there's a great white shark! A big one—in the shallows!"

Ralph looks puzzled. "What were you doing in the shallows? That's not on the route."

"I took a wrong turn."

Rick and Donny are giggling bubbles into the water. "Hammer-vision gone wrong again?" says Rick.

"If you don't believe me, why don't you come and have a look for yourself?" I press my nose right into Rick's face.

He looks a bit shocked. "All right. Show us."

I lead the way, pulling Ralph by the fin, and feeling Joe cling to my tail with several of his many tentacles.

Rick and Donny follow, but at a safe distance. They're not as brave as they pretend to be.

We burst out of the coral marsh and head up toward the shallows. The weather up above the sea seems to be getting worse. There are lots of clouds now, and the water is full of shadows. It's going to be hard to spot the . . .

But yes—right above us—the *huge* shadow!

"There it is!"

Ralph, Joe, Rick, and Donny look to where I'm pointing.

And that's when the sun comes out from behind the bank of clouds.

458

And then I see Donny, Rick, and Ralph
start to laugh.

Joe just giggles out of his rear.

Huh?

I look back up.

Oh.

No.

In the bright sunlight, the shark is revealed in all its glory.

Its pink glory.

Its plastic glory.

Its girly pink plastic shark-shaped glory.

It's a raft. One of those plastic blow-up things used by the leggy air-breathers to float on the water.

It's not a shark.

And now I'm so uncool, you could fry sea-cucumber fritters on my face.

Ralph stops laughing when he sees my shoulders slump. Then he pokes Joe, who immediately stops tooting.

Rick swims so close to me, I can count the go-faster stripes on his track-suit. "Nice one, Harry. You can't even tell a great white shark from a raft. Wait until everyone at school hears about this!"

Rick and Donny high-fin, and swim
away laughing.

I can't believe I've been so dopey.
Again!

CHAPTER 5

When school finally finishes, I sneak past the field, darting behind clumps of sea plants. I just want to get away as quickly as possible without being seen. Rick, Donny, Ralph, and Joe are playing finball with some other kids from class. Normally I'd stop and play too.

Not tonight.

Not after the day I've had.

Everywhere I went today, in every class, fish have been pulling my fin about the raft—even Mrs. Shelby. When Mr. Gape, our basking-shark librarian, came in, she said, "Now don't worry, Harry, there's no need to be scared. I know he looks like another type of shark. . . . "

You know you're in trouble when *teachers* are laughing at you.

I slink away from school and the happy sounds of the finballers. Rick has just scored a curling net-ripper and everyone is going crazy cheering. The dolphin twins are singing "Ra ra ra, Rick!" like cheerleaders on the sideline.

Well, that's okay.

I don't need friends. I don't need anyone to play finball with.

I bet G-White doesn't care about friends. Why would he, now he's a famous wrestler, movie star, and rapper?

And one day, I'm gonna be just like that.

H-Hed. That's what I'll call myself. That's a great name for a . . .

Sigh.

Yeah.

465

It's *totally* awful. I can't even come up with a good rapper's name. I might as well just give up.

When I get home, Mom's bustling around the kitchen making snacks. I hang up my book bag and coat, thinking that at least today can't get any worse.

"Oh, good!" Mom calls out when she sees me. "I need you to go to the newsstand." She goes over to her finbag and takes out some money. "I didn't get a chance to pick up my *True Love Forever* magazine earlier, and it always sells out really quickly. Can you go out and buy me one while I finish my snack?"

Why is it that whenever I think a day can't get any worse, it always does?

Now, hammer-vision-fail-raft-spotter-boy is going to have to swim to the newsstand and ask for a copy of *True Love Forever* magazine. Knowing  my luck, Cora and Pearl will be there, filming it on their SeaPhones to upload straight onto CrewTube.

But if this doesn't go wrong, then something tomorrow is bound to.

So what's the point in fighting it?

I put out my fin for the money.

"Make sure it's this week's though," Mom says. "The one with the bright pink cover and the free Twilight Trout Pout lipstick."

Great.

I swim out of the house and off to the main road, my heart nose-diving with doom.

I can tell everyone's looking at me as I swim slowly along. I've been all over the news for two days now—I'm the laughing stock of Shark Point.

A prawn whizzing by on a

skateboard asks me if I'm on my way to the optician's to get my hammer-vision tested.

I ignore him.

A hermit crab puts his pincers over his head in an arch. "Look out, I'm a great white!" He laughs so hard, his shell falls off.

I ignore him, too. If this goes on much longer, I'll be ignoring all of Shark Point.

Thankfully, there's no one else around when I get to the newsstand, since it's on a quiet side street. The store after the newsstand is the Wet Pet Shop. Usually when I come here, I press my hammer up at the window to look at the kittenfish in their tanks. But today I can't be bothered. I just want to buy the magazine and get the embarrassment over and done with.

The Wet Pet Shop door is locked and there's a big "Gone Fishin" sign hanging on it. No wonder the street is so quiet—if the Wet Pet Shop is closed, there's hardly any reason for anyone to come down here.

Finally, my luck seems to be changing. I'm just about to take the magazine from the newsstand when . . .

Grrrrrrrrrrrrr!

Wow, my stomach is rumbling like crazy. I hadn't even realized I was hungry.

Grrrrrrrrrrrrrrrrrrrrrr!

I don't think it's ever rumbled so loud in my life.

Grrrrrrrrrrrrrrrrrrrrrrrrrrrrrrrrr!!!

But hang on a minute, I don't think the low growling, grumbling, rumbling noise is coming from my stomach after all.

PING!

My hammer-vision starts going off.

PING!

PING!!!

"Yeah, right. So what is it this time? A rubber pacifier with teeth?" I say.

PING!

PING!!

PING!!!

I have a look around on the main road, but I can't see anything wrong. It must be COMPLETELY broken. Great. I'm a hammerhead with no hammer-vision.

Annoyed, I glance back the way I came and nearly do a double fin-flip in shock. This time, there *IS* a great white!

It's huge, it looks super mean, and it's hanging above the Wet Pet Shop, staring down at the window. But it's not about to go "Awwwwwwww" at the kittenfish. It's licking its lips and it's

Grrrrrrrrrrrrring, getting ready to go in for the kill!

I have to do something! I have to say something!

"H-h-h-h-hello. H-h-h-h-h-h-how are you?"

Yes, I know it's nonsense and I sound like I'm terrified. But that's because I am terrified, and I don't know what else to say.

In the window, the kittenfish are trying to hide under each other.

"Shut it, kid, can't you see I'm busy?" the great white growls. "I'm about to have my snack. Shouldn't you be going home to get yours?"

474

The great white starts dropping slowly in the water, licking his lips and winding up his tail.

"You don't get your snack from the Wet Pet Shop." My heart starts beating a million times too fast in my chest.

The great white looks at me with his big black eyes.

"Where else am I going to get live kittenfish? I love the way they wriggle as they go down my throat."

The kittenfish start getting more panicky in their tank, swimming around in circles, squeaking and mewing. This just seems to make the great white

even more excited. He opens his mouth and gnashes his teeth.

I look around for anyone else who can come and help. But the street is still deserted.

I dart back up to the main road, desperate to tell someone, *anyone*, what's going on. I swim up to a whale and her kids.

"Quick! Down there! There's a great white!" I gasp.

The whale just smiles and pats me on the head. "Yes, of course there is, dear. I don't think you're going to get us with that one again. Nice try though!"

"But—"

The whale just swims on, with her kids finning their noses at me.

Oh no!

I dodge some turtle-cars and go up to an octopus who is looking in a jeweller's window at eight-holed engagement rings.

"Help!" I shout, shaking him by the tentacle. "There's a great white at the Wet Pet Shop! He's about to eat the kittenfish!"

The octopus turns and looks at me. "Forget it, kid. I heard all about your great white prank on the jellyfishion." He blows ink in my face and goes back to looking in the window.

I dart up and down the street, looking

477

for someone else to tell. I'm near the
side street when I hear . . .

CRASH!

It's coming from the Wet Pet Shop.

The great white must be starting his attack!

CRASH!

I start swimming faster. I can't leave the kittenfish to him. I have to do something to stop them from becoming the great white's snack—even if it means I end up becoming his dessert!

CHAPTER 6

I know that this really isn't the best time to make a list. But a list of things that make me happy will make me feel less scared. As the great white winds himself up to smash into the Wet Pet Shop door again, I start listing like crazy in my head.

1. **Kelp krispies.** I like them! I'm so close to the great white now, I can see a piece of seaweed trapped between his teeth.

2. **Ralph.** He's great. I like him! I'm so close to the great white now, I can see a tattoo on his dorsal fin saying: **FIGHT 4 THE RIGHT TO BITE.**

3. **Joe.** He's great too! I'm so close to the great white now, I'm actually in between him and the shop!

4. **And Mom and Dad.** I love them, too! I really, really love them!

I've reached the end of my list.

"STOP!" I shout as loudly and as scarily as I can.

The great white is all coiled up, ready to smash into the door of the Wet Pet Shop for a final time, as the hinges are just about to give way. He pauses for a moment. He stares at me with his huge, black, mean-looking eyes.

"You again? What did I tell you a minute ago, kid? Get out of the way or you're in big trouble."

"Kittenfish? What kind of cowardly shark eats kittenfish? Well, obviously a coward with all the bravery of a dead haddock." I cannot believe what just came out of my mouth. Now I'm dessert for sure.

"What did you say?" growls the great white.

Oh well, if I'm going to be a great white's dessert I suppose I've got nothing left to lose. "Are you deaf as well as a coward? Or just *out to lunch*?"

Oh. MY. COD!

"GRRRRRRRRRRRRRRRRRRRRRR-
RRRRRRRRRRRRRRRRRRRRRR!!!!!"

The great white lets his wound-up tail go and leaps straight at me.

But that's exactly what I wanted. "Catch me if you can!" I yell, and I'm off too.

Zoooooooooooooooooooooooooooom!

PING!!! PING!!!

I know, hammer-vision! I know!

I shoot off toward the main road, knowing the great white will follow.

My hammer-vision clicks automatically to ESCAPE MODE. I hope this time it doesn't let me down.

ZOOOOM! I shoot round the corner.

A turtle taxi screeches to a halt as I shoot on to the road.

"Watch where you're going!" screams the taxi driver, waving his flipper with anger.

"GREAT WHITE!" I scream as I dart over him.

"Just you wait 'til I tell your dad the mayor about this!" the driver shouts. "You're going to be grounded for . . . for . . . for . . . "

The great white zooms out of the side street after me, and the turtle's jaw drops down in shock. "For . . . for . . . for . . . It's a GREAT WHITE!"

"That's what I *said*!" I cry as I shoot down the street with the great white snapping at my tail. As I go, faces change from smiles and laughter to total terror as they see what's snarling away behind me.

Fish dive into store doorways, squids slide under turtles. Outside

Guppy's Grocery Store boxes of sea fruit get smashed into the air by my hammer-head, and telephone poles get knocked over by the wild flapping of the great white's huge tail.

I can tell from the currents in the water that he's gaining on me.

"I'm gonna chew you up and spit you out, boy!" the great white shouts.

"You've got to catch me first!" I yell behind me.

My hammer-vision escape mode is pinging away, warning me of any obstacles. A turtle bus from Crabton pulls out in front of me and I squeeze under it. The great white has to go over.

I swim off the street out toward the Point. A school of minnows is returning from a class outing. I skirt around the side of the group. The great white is too big to swerve that quickly and he ploughs on straight ahead. Luckily, the teacher, an old hermit crab with little glasses and a knitted sweater, has pushed all the young fish aside, and the great white just sails through.

I'm kicking and kicking, turning this way and that. But the great white is still gaining on me. I'm trying to think of ways to shake him off.

I turn a sick full 180 half-fin, and barrel

into a reverse tail-endy. This sends the great white flying over my head, and suddenly I'm heading away from the Point in the opposite direction.

I'm starting to get tired now, so I know I won't be able to keep this up for long.

"Come here!" the great white bellows, finally managing to change direction and follow me again.

I don't know what I'm going to do. I've managed to lead the great white away from town, but now what?

PING!

My hammer-vision is looking

waaaaaaaaaaaaaaay ahead. It zooms the school playground right into view.

I can see Rick and the others still playing finball, and my hammer-vision super senses send me faint sounds of Cora and Pearl, still cheerleading.

I can't go right, because that will take me over the coral marsh.

I can't go left, because that will take me out into the wide ocean.

I can't go back, because the great white will just eat me!

I've got to go on, but that means I'm going to lead the great white . . . *straight to my friends!*

"Great white!" I scream as the play-ground gets closer and closer.

I can see Rick about to take one of his fancy-pants free kicks with the fin-ball. Everyone else is concentrating on that, rather than me and the great white shooting toward them at top speed!

"GREAT WHITE!" I yell again at the top of my voice.

"Pipe down, Harry! Can't you see I'm concentrating?" Rick calls over his shoulder. He continues lining up the ball.

We're almost there. I can feel the vibrations in the water as the great white's jaws chomp after my tail. I can

492

feel the hot, hungry breath blowing from his gills.

What am I going to do?

Rick takes a float back. He's ready to kick.

Ralph is floating between the goal posts, wearing goalkeeping gloves on his fins. He's focusing hard on Rick, getting ready to try and save the ball.

"OUCH!"

The great white is nipping at my flukes.

"I can almost taste you, kid!" he snarls.

Ralph looks over Rick's head—straight at me and the great white.

"Great white!" he yells.

"You won't fool me with lame-o tricks like your goofy friend," Rick sneers.

"Great white!" calls Joe. ***Pop pop pop pop pop pop,*** calls his rear.

"Oh, zip it!" Rick yells.

"Ra ra ra," the dolphin twins sing. "Ra ra raaaaggghhhhh!" the dolphin twins scream as they turn to look at what Ralph and Joe are looking at. Me—being chased by a great big great white.

Rick starts swishing his tail angrily. "It's my free kick. Stop trying to ruin it!"

"Rick!" yells Donny, pointing wildly with his fin. "LOOK!"

And finally Rick *does* look.

And then he just about breaks the sea-speed record for hiding behind twin dolphins with your rear tooting like a motorboat!

"GREAT WHITE!" he screams as he flies behind Pearl and Cora.

"I know!" I scream back as I skim low across the field. And then an idea pings into my head even louder than my hammer-vision. I start waving my fins madly at Ralph in the goal.

"Ralph! Get out the way!" I yell.

Ralph dives to the left, covering his head with his fins.

I've got just one chance for my plan to work. I head straight for the goal, kicking as hard and as fast as I can. The great white's hot gill-breath is sending shivers up my spine.

The goal posts come up really fast. I hold out my fins and curl my whole body into a sharky body-knot. I grab the top of the post with my fin and hope that my speed will be enough to carry me around. It is. I spin around the post, up over the crossbar, and as I come around I flick out both flukes of my tail as hard as I can.

CRACK!!!

The great white's nose connects perfectly with my tail-flick. The nose is where great whites keep all their most sensitive hunting sensors and delicate S.H.A.R.K.D.A.R. equipment. It's also the most vulnerable place on a great white's body. If you're ever facing a great white, hit him as hard as you can on the nose.

BOIIIIIIIIIIIIIIINNNNNNNNNNGG!

The great white's eyes snap shut and his body goes limp. He's traveling so fast that his whole body flies forward, knocking me aside as he shoots right into the goal.

ONE-ZERO HARRY!

The great white is completely unconscious as he floats in the water, but he won't be for long. I swim up, unhook the

net from the crossbar, and drape the net over him. Then, grabbing the net in my teeth, I swim around and around until he is totally tied up.

Done!

"Yaaaaaaaaaaaaaaaay!" cry the dolphin twins.

"Yesssssssssssssssssssssssssss!" cry Ralph and Joe.

"Has it gone yet?" whimpers Rick, still hiding behind Pearl and Cora.

And then it seems like the whole town is crowding on to the finball field, coming to see what's happened. At the head of the crowd are Mom and Dad.

Mom throws herself at me and gives me a massive hug. "Starfish! You've saved us all!"

For the first time ever, I'm not embarrassed by Mom calling me starfish. But that's probably because everyone is pointing at the great white trapped in the net and cheering like crazy.

Cheering ME!

Dad high-fins me, then raises my fin like I'm a champion wrestler. "I'm so proud of you, son," he says with a smile.

Ralph, Joe, Cora, Pearl, and even Donny the Dogfish are pushing their way through the crowd toward me. Ralph and

Joe can't stop smiling. Cora and Pearl are snapping away with the cameras on their SeaPhones. Donny is clapping and cheering! In the background I can see

Rick getting off the seabed and dusting himself off with his fins. He doesn't look happy at the attention I'm getting.

But I don't care. It's AWESOME.

"Harry's hammer-vision saved us all!" Dad shouts, and from the clapping and cheering it seems like the whole town agrees.

I can't believe it. Just this morning I was so down in the dumps that I wanted the seabed to swallow me whole. Now I'm on top of the ocean!

As everyone gathers around me, high-finning me and slapping me on the back, I realize something so shocking, it makes my goggly eyes spin. Ever since I can remember, I've wanted to be a great white, but I'm a hammerhead who *outwitted* a great white. It's not just G-White who has the shark factor.

I've got BUCKETS FULL of it!

Meet Harry and the Shark Point gang. . . .

HARRY

Species:
hammerhead shark

You'll spot him . . .
using his special
hammer-vision

Favorite thing:
his Gregor the Gnasher
poster

Most likely to say:
"I wish I was a great white."

Most embarrassing moment: when Mom called him
her "little starfish" in front of all his friends

RALPH

Species:

pilot fish

You'll spot him . . .

eating the food from

between

Harry's teeth!

Favorite thing: shrimp Pop-Tarts

Most likely to say: "So, Harry, what's for

breakfast today?"

Most embarrassing moment: eating too much cake

on Joe's birthday. His face was COVERED in pink

plankton icing.

JOE

Species: jellyfish

You'll spot him . . . hiding behind Ralph and Harry, or behind his own tentacles

Favorite thing: his cave, since it's nice and safe

Most likely to say: "If we do this, we're going to end up as fish food. . . ."

Most embarrassing moment: whenever his rear goes *toot*, which is when he's scared. Which is all the time.

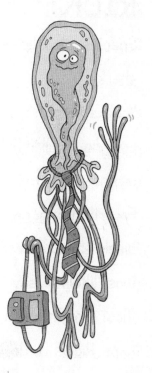

RICK

Species: blacktip reef shark

You'll spot him . . . bullying smaller fish or showing off

Favorite thing: his black leather jacket

Most likely to say: "Last one there's a sea snail!"

Most embarrassing moment: none. Rick's far too cool to get embarrassed.

Shark Bites

SHARK BITES

Sharks have been swimming in the world's oceans for more than 400 million years.

There are more than four hundred different species of shark, from the giant hammerhead to the goblin shark.

Sharks do not have bones. They are cartilaginous fish, which means their skeletons are made of cartilage, not bone. Cartilage is a type of connective tissue that is softer than bone. Humans have cartilage in their ears and nose.

The shortfin mako is the fastest shark in the ocean. It can swim in bursts as fast as forty-six miles per hour.

The whale shark is the largest shark in the sea. It can grow to be as long as sixty feet.

SHARK BITES

There are nine species of hammerhead shark, including scoophead and bonnethead.

A wild hammerhead can live for twenty to thirty years.

Hammerheads live in moderate and tropical warm waters.

The largest hammerhead is the great hammerhead, which can weigh about five hundred pounds.

The eyes of the hammerhead shark, which are on each side of its head, allow the hammerhead to look around an area more quickly than other sharks. It also has special sensors across its head that help it scan for food.

Hammerheads eat stingrays, bony fish, crabs, lobsters, squid, and many other sea creatures.

SHARK BITES

Hammerhead sharks have a great sense of smell and are able to locate food easily.

The blacktip reef shark is bluish-gray in color and is usually found in the coral reefs and shallow lagoons of the tropical Indian and Pacific Oceans.

The pilot fish is carnivorous (eats meat, other animals) and not only follows whales, sharks, and turtles, but also ships so that it can feed on parasites and leftover scraps of food. The pilot fish came by its name because it was thought to lead, or "pilot," larger fishes to sources of food.

SHARK BITES

Jellyfish have been on the earth for millions and millions of years. They were here before dinosaurs.

Bottlenose dolphins are not fish; they are mammals. They breathe air, just like humans do.

The longest living creature on Earth is the red sea urchin. Some have lived more than two hundred years.

The largest coral reef on Earth is the Great Barrier Reef, located in the Coral Sea near Australia.

SHARK BiTES

The dorsal fin is the main fin that is located on the back of a fish or marine (relating to the sea) animal.

Plankton can be plants or animals, but since they can't swim, they have to rely on the tides and currents of the ocean in order to move.

Sea cows are also known as manatees. They never leave the water, but since they are mammals, sea cows must come to the surface to breathe air.

Minnows can live in both salt water and fresh water.

SHARK BITES

The basking shark is the second-largest fish in existence. Only the whale shark is bigger. Their mouths can be more than three feet in width!

An electric eel does not have teeth. It can grow up to nine feet in length.

Starfish are also known as sea stars. Although most starfish have five arms, some can have as many as twelve!

Piranha are freshwater fish mostly found in the waters of South America. They are carnivorous, which means they eat meat.

Most great white sharks are between thirteen and sixteen feet long and weigh from 1,500 to 2,450 pounds.

The teeth of great white sharks are razor sharp.

ABOUT THE AUTHORS

DAVY OCEAN has traveled the seven seas in search of good seafaring shanties and fishy tales. He currently resides in a small fishing town that overlooks Shark Point and allows him uninterrupted access to the antics of a small community of hammerhead sharks and its fellow ocean neighbors.

AARON BLECHA is an artist who designs funny characters, animates silly cartoons, and illustrates humorous books. His work incudes illustrations for the bestselling book series George Brown, Class Clown. Originally from the United States, Aaron now lives with his family by the south English seaside.